Knotted

A M/F Demon Werewolf Romance

Yarn & Monsters
Book 4

Sabrina Cross

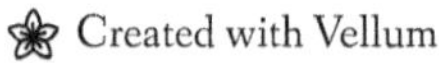 Created with Vellum

For Sasha & Melinda,
Neither of you know it, but you're the reason the
series exists.

Author's Note

This is a sentient object romance. Humans will be getting it on with sentient objects. Don't worry, everyone is gleefully consenting.

If you read the last three sentences and think that's not for you, that's okay. There is still time to put this book down and walk away. No one will blame you. It's the sane thing to do.

But if you're going to stick around please be aware of the following: Graphic sexual activity (oral, vaginal, anal), sex with a half-turned wolf-man, light dub-con, light degradation, threats of violence (not between main characters), low self-worth in female main character

If you feel I am missing anything please reach out to me at authorsabrinacross@gmail.com and let me know. A complete list can be found at www.sabrinacross.com

Chapter One

There was something fundamentally wrong with me.

It was the only reason I could think of for finding myself at home on a Friday night cuddling a two-foot-tall crochet werewolf and wondering why it hadn't been possessed by a demon.

Not that I actually wanted it to be possessed by a demon. It was just I was ten months into a deal with the devil and I was supposed to be assigned a demon by now.

It definitely had nothing to do with my three closest friends happily paired up and off the dating scene. Or my most recent attempt at dating, finding the love of *his* life at my cousin's wedding last month.

I was happy for them. I really, really was. It was great for all of them and frankly, every one of them deserved happiness. But a large part of me was sad for myself.

Ten months ago, I had talked my friends into

doing a love spell. It had mostly been a joke as I entered my twenty-ninth year of life. I felt cosmic intervention was the only way I was going to find a good relationship.

It was ridiculous and silly. None of us had taken it seriously. Fern, Jasmine, and Clover had humored me. A true love spell? It was a joke. A lark.

Except, it wasn't.

It wasn't a normal spell either. It was signing a blood deal with the devil. He would help us find true love, but if we couldn't find our soul mates within a year, he got our souls.

One by one, my friends had been given a demon guardian. The demon was there to keep them safe and whole while they searched for their soul mates. And one by one, my friends fell in love with the demons they had been given.

I was certain it was part of the devil's game. Instead of unwilling souls, he was given three women willing to follow their demon lovers into Hell. Honestly, you had to hand it to the guy. Especially because my friends had never been happier.

I was totally prepared to fall in love with whatever demon arrived at my door. Or, inside my crochet werewolf, rather. Except, it had been ten months since we'd done the spell, and the first demon arrived. And I still hadn't seen so much of a hint of demon.

My friends insisted it would be okay, but I knew better. There were fewer than two months until my birthday and the anniversary of our deal. In two months, I would go to Hell. And there wasn't a damn thing I could do to stop it.

Oh, I'd tried. I'd reached out to every witch, pagan, druid, mythology scholar, and occultist I could find, but none of them had heard of such a thing. Most of them had assumed I was some kind of crazy. Apparently, they didn't appreciate their spiritual beliefs being mocked by my wild tales of real demons.

Funny that.

"I wonder if I'll be able to take you to Hell with me." I told the stuffed werewolf. The thing was silly. A grey, white, and black wolf with blue "jeans" it's ragged hems and his button-down red shirt was raggedy and ripped. It was hysterical, and I was blown away by Clover's skill with a hook.

"Good night, buddy." I turned off the light and snuggled under my duvet with my arm around the wolf.

Just a few weeks to go before my chit came due. It was fine. There was still time.

"It would help if you'd get possessed already. If nothing else, I really, really need to get laid."

Chapter Two

The first thing I noticed was the heat. It was mid-June and summer had sprung, so waking up warm wasn't abnormal. But this wasn't June warm. This was late-July heat wave at high noon-hot. I kicked the blanket, but it didn't move. Something wrapped around my waist, keeping it, and me, in place.

My eyes flew open as I turned toward the furnace. Where my stuffed werewolf had lain last night was a giant black beast.

I slapped a hand to my mouth to keep the scream in. The beast appeared to be sleeping. The last thing I wanted to do was startle it awake. The claws that rested on my hip were long and sharp. My stomach clenched, imagining the damage they could do to me.

Taking a deep breath, I took my hand off my mouth and began scooting slowly toward the edge of my queen-sized bed. The beast's breathing stayed steady as I slowly slid out from under its large, furry limb.

I had one foot on the floor and had nearly freed myself when the beast let out a snuffling-snort sound and his claws tensed over my stomach.

"Where are you going, love?" The voice was a grumbling-growl. A deep vibration in the chest of the beast. The claws I'd nearly escaped flexed, and I froze, praying this wasn't it. This wasn't the way I died.

Instead of ripping my insides out, the large paw wrapped around my center and yanked me back onto the bed and up against the furry furnace. It pulled me until I was flush against it, my back to its front. Those long claws rested on my stomach. Its snout snuffled into my hair and brushed against my neck. I shuddered at the feeling.

"Mmmm, isn't this better?" The growl vibrated through me. My pulse raced through every cell of my body. I fought to keep my breathing even as it nuzzled against me. "You smell even sweeter than I imagined. All softness and fear. I could eat you up."

A warm, wet tongue licked up the back of my neck. I shuddered in revulsion. Oh gods, this was going to be how I died. I was going to be eaten by a giant hellhound. Maybe this was how Lucifer was claiming my soul.

"You can't eat me. I still have two months

left." It was an asinine thing to say. Of course, this giant beast could eat me and there was nothing I could do to stop it. A point made very clear when the claws pressed into my stomach. Not enough to cut into my skin, but enough to feel the sharp points against my flesh.

The beast laughed; the loud booming sound shook through me. It practically howled with it. After what felt like a century, the beast settled down and snuggled his snout into the crook of my neck.

"Oh, love, you are a delight." The claws on my stomach ran down over the curve of my belly and up again, dragging my shirt with it. The claws left red marks on my skin. I watched as the beast scratched me and willed myself to not react.

It didn't seem interested in killing me, but it was toying with me. I wouldn't give it a reason to change its mind. At least, not until I was free of its grasp.

"You're going to be a good girl, now, right? If I let you go, you're not going to run."

I shook my head, unable to speak. My eyes locked on the claws gently flexing against my soft, rounded stomach. It would take so little pressure for it to rip into me. I was prepared to agree to anything if it meant freeing myself from the cage of its body.

Slowly, the beast released me. I scrambled off the bed and back against the wall. There was nowhere to go. The door was on the other side of the bed. I doubted I would be able to make it there before the beast stopped me.

The beast sat up, swinging oddly canine legs over the side of the bed. It rubbed its claws through its hair in what could have been an endearing gesture from a man, but was mostly unsettling coming from the hulking giant.

It was a classic wolfman. Both humanoid and canine in appearance, its whole body covered in thick, wavy black fur. Its eyes were black, the whites standing out starkly against all of the darkness. I suddenly desperately wondered if it had a tail.

That final thought broke me, and I burst out laughing. I couldn't help it. This whole situation was so ridiculous. Laughter wheezed out of me and I doubled over with my butt against the wall and laughed.

"Oh, lovely," the beast growled. "The human is mad."

I drew myself up to my full height, a very not impressive or intimidating five-two, and wiped tears from my eyes. I wasn't mad. My life was insane. I was having a perfectly logical reaction to a literal werewolf in my bed. I told him so.

"You chose the form, love. I'm here to fulfill your fantasy." It looked down at itself and huffed. "You humans, so little imagination."

"I chose..." The words hit me and I looked around for the werewolf doll Clover had made me. It was still there, on the floor, peeking out from the end of the bed. "But you're not in the toy."

The beast stood and shook itself, a hint of tail peeked around his leg and I mentally applauded myself for not breaking into hysterics again. It drew itself up, up, up. The tips of its ears just inches from the ceiling.

"What do you take me for? I am no mere demon." It stepped forward, caging me in between it and the wall. "I am not limited by the same rules as those who came before me."

A clawed paw landed on the wall above my shoulder. The beast loomed over me and grinned a terrifying, toothy grin. I took a shuddering breath and searched for a way out. But the beast filled my entire eyeline.

The only way out was through. I could do this.

"Okay, so you're like a super-demon? Epic demon? Oh shit, are you Lucifer?"

The demon huffed. I couldn't tell if the sound was amused, or annoyed. But its paw didn't move, and I allowed myself to relax an inch.

"I am the demon lord Asmodeus. I am the commander of legions." Its other paw landed on the wall, caging me in. The beast leaned down and settled its muzzle next to my face. "And, Violet, I've come for you."

There was a small part of me thrilled over the dark, gravelly voice stating he came for me. It was a very small part. The tiny part that still wanted to believe in fairy tales and happy endings and dreams come true.

That part was incredibly stupid. As was the part that immediately had its hackles rise and act as though I would with anyone who tried to lay claim to me. I reached my hands up and shoved him back, using my arms to slam his hands down from the wall and giving me a moment to slide out from between him and the wall and into the open room.

"Are you fucking kidding me?" I snapped at him.

He roared and spun, reaching out for me.

I sidestepped back and away. I wasn't running. He'd done nothing to harm me and I had a sick feeling I knew what this was. I wasn't in much danger. But I was pissed.

"Seriously, you come into my house, climb into my bed, while I am sleeping and what, think we're going to ride off into the sunset together? Are you fucking delusional?"

"I could have just taken you. Claimed what is already mine."

"My soul may be yours, in two months, but you'll never have my mind or my body. You don't get to claim those."

A hand came out to grab a long section of hair. The move was gentle and yet somehow threatening. Sharp claws brushed through the strands, and he watched it fall through his hand. "We shall see, love." With that oh-so-comforting statement, he released me and ambled out of my room. "What do you have to eat around here? I'm starving."

I stared after him, completely incredulous. I had begun to believe whatever demon was sent my way might be my soulmate, but there was no way in Hell I was ever going to fall in love with that beast.

Chapter Three

I was hiding in my bedroom from a demon and I didn't know what to do about it. I'd already changed into a comfy blue sundress, secured my pink hair back into a braid, changed the bedding, sorted through the chair of clothing, either putting them back in the dresser or putting them in the dirty laundry as needed.

My phone was plugged in down in the kitchen, and my ereader was in my work bag. I didn't have a TV in my room. I was sitting on my bed fidgeting with the skirt of my dress, trying to decide the best way to handle this situation.

"Come on, Vi, you're better than this." I told myself, trying to get the gumption to get up and leave my bedroom. Not that I thought the closed door would keep the beast out if he decided he wanted in. It hadn't stopped him last night when he'd made his way into my bed.

I was still so angry about it. About him invading my space and stealing my sense of safety.

The smell of him, a smoky amber, had seeped into my bedding and had me ripping the sheets off. They were in a tangled heap on the floor next to my laundry basket. I would have to take the comforter to the laundromat, but there was no way I could sleep with his scent surrounding me.

"Okay, Vi. You can't hide here forever." I toyed with the end of my braid and then took a deep breath. I would not be a prisoner in my room, in my own home. I would go get a cup of coffee and a bowl of cereal and then go do my normal Saturday chores. Surely, I could come up with an answer to the demon problem while I was gone.

My plan went sideways when I made it to the dining room to find a full breakfast spread set out on my table. There were eggs, sausage, bacon, pancakes, toast, orange juice, a carafe of coffee sat steaming on a heat pad. How the hell had he done this? I knew for a fact I didn't have any of it available in my house. My fridge was pathetically empty when I went to bed last night.

"About time you stopped hiding. I thought I was going to have to come get you." I whirled around to see the beast come out of the kitchen carrying two plates with mugs and glasses balanced on top with silverware sticking out of the cups. A part of me wondered how he managed to carry it with the awkward gait his half-canine legs caused without dumping anything.

"I wasn't hiding." I snapped. A clear lie. "I was cleaning."

"You keep telling yourself that." He passed by me and walked to the table. "Are you going to sit?"

No. I did not want to sit down.

My stomach grumbled audibly. The beast sent an indisputable smirk in my direction. I could have ignored it, but my stomach was empty and the food looked damn good. It would be a damn shame to waste it.

"How?" I asked, gesturing to the table as I waited for him to sit before picking the chair farthest away. Another smirk.

"Being a demon lord comes with some privileges." The look he shot me had me flashing hot. Fire was banked in those black eyes. And I hated myself just a little for being affected by it.

I looked away and took a plate, loading it up with food before smothering all of it in maple syrup. Real maple syrup. Not the imitation stuff I usually bought because it was cheaper.

I forked up a giant bite of pancake and froze. I knew better than to accept food from the fae, but I had never heard any lore about food from a demon lord. It was probably a bad idea.

"It's not poisoned." Asmodeus said, scooping up a forkful of eggs and shoving it into his mouth.

"What's not poison for a demon might be fatal for a human. You could be trying to kill me." I set the fork down and was about to push away from the table when he grabbed my wrist. Claws wrapping carefully around the delicate skin. It was a firm hold, but not painful.

"You will come to no harm by my hands." His voice was low and serious and caused tension to curl in my belly.

"What about one of your minions? If they made it and delivered it, then it wouldn't be your hands." It was a little convoluted, but I could trust nothing.

Your life is safe from me and mine." He stared me down. I couldn't escape from his gaze. "I've waited so long for you, my love. I would hardly let you come to harm now I've found you."

I didn't know what to make of it. This hulking beastly demon knew nothing about me. I didn't care if he'd been watching me since we'd done the spell, it was hardly enough to know me. The last ten months had been wasted on pointless dates and futile searches for information on how to escape the deal we'd unwittingly made. It was hardly a true representation of who I was as a person.

"You don't know me." I said, pulling my arm free from his grasp. "You don't know anything about me. Whoever you think you've been waiting for, it isn't me. And I'm not your anything."

I pushed away from the table and the feast there and left the room. A large part of me had expected the demon to follow me and stop me. And if a small part of me was disappointed he didn't, well, we wouldn't think about that small, stupid part.

Chapter Four

"**P**hinarax! I'm going to string you up by your balls and play pinata on your ass!" I yelled when I walked into Jasmine's house. Jasmine and the girls were at a birthday party, but Phin was home and he was the one most likely to actually answer my questions. Candy may be a slave for Clover, but she was hardly warm and cuddly with the rest of us. Jax wasn't capable of taking much of anything seriously. Phin was the most together of the demons and the one most likely to know about my new demon foe.

"Violet," the tall demon came down the stairs with a wry smile. "I see you're as sweet as usual. For what do I earn such threats of violence?"

"Asmodeus." The bright red demon, who usually moved with easy grace, stumbled. He recovered quickly but I'd seen it and it tightened the ball of tension in my gut.

"So, it's true." He stopped next to me and gestured toward the kitchen. I followed him in silence, questions swirling around my mind. "We'd wondered, of course. But he so rarely comes topside. I wasn't sure anything would drive him out of his corner of Hell anymore."

I lifted myself onto the barstool and accepted the cup of coffee Phin offered. It was black, which was barely tolerable, but I wanted the caffeine. Phin set a plate of muffins on the island before drawing up a stool next to me.

Phin was so comically domestic. From the moment he arrived, he'd been taking care of the house and he never stopped. He was the one who cooked and cleaned and handled laundry. Jasmine told me he even planned to take over child chauffeur duties when school started again in the fall. He was everything my friend needed and everything I wanted and hoped for. And while I was so happy Jasmine had him, it made the beast in my house a cruel blow.

He tried to feed you. That tiny, annoying voice in my brain said.

It was probably poison. I shot back. Not wanting to talk myself out of being angry.

"He's why you're here," I said. It wasn't a question. It was something I'd put together on my drive over and I knew in my bones I was right. Asmodeus had sent the other demons here. He'd made sure to manipulate them and my friends.

"He is my demon lord." Phin hedged. "He was why I was sent, but Jasmine is what keeps me here."

"Explain." I needed to know. I needed to

understand. Nothing about this demon deal/curse/spell made any kind of sense. There was nothing I could find to explain why it had happened the way it had happened. There was nothing in the spell book that should have tied us to a demon deal. I'd read it cover to cover and done so much research and nothing made sense.

"It's complicated."

"Lots of things are. Talk to me like I'm five and asking how babies are made." Phin shuddered, and I bared my teeth in a feral grin. I knew Jasmine's youngest had posed that question recently, and Phin was traumatized by the conversation.

Phin spun his coffee cup between his hands, claws scraping annoyingly against the ceramic. After what felt like an eternity, he took a deep breath and nodded.

"There are two kinds of demons. There are born demons and made demons. The born demons are very rare and very old. No new demons have been born in a millennium. Those demons are part of a caste system. Those of us turned into demons serve a born demon. Asmodeus is a demon lord; he answers to Lucifer directly."

"What causes a demon to be made?" I asked before I could think of it. "Never mind. That's none of my business."

Whatever had led to Phin being turned into a demon, he was a good man, a good partner, and a good father figure. It was all I needed to know about him.

"Thank you." Phin took a large drink of coffee and went on. "There are few things that can unmake or release a demon. Demon lords can unmake a demon, which destroys their soul entirely. Poof, out of existence. They can also release a demon from their service. It doesn't happen often, but it leaves the demon free from overlord control."

"Were you released?" I needed to know. I needed to know that the demon my friend loved wasn't going to disappear on her one day and leave her heartbroken.

"Of a sort." He was back to spinning his mug between his hands. "Technically, I am still in the service of Asmodeus. But the oversight is kind of like being on parole. So long as I keep out of trouble, he doesn't care much what I'm doing."

I picked up a muffin for something to do with my hands as I thought about that. It didn't mean Phin, or the others were free, but hopefully it meant my friends were safe for now. My shoulders sagged in relief as I thought about them living their happy ever afters. It also meant I was probably right in assuming this was how the devil would claim us. I thought about asking Phin his opinion, but there was something else I needed to know more.

"What did you mean when you said it's true? What's true?" I picked the blueberries out of the top of the muffin and dropped them on a napkin I snagged from the center of the island. I liked blueberries, but my stomach was too upset to eat and I needed to keep my hands busy or I was going to lose my mind.

"There's been chatter about your demon deal. Thousands of offers come through every day and the demon lords ignore them. They really don't care about the daily happenings on Earth. They're too busy dealing with politics in Hell and keeping their legions in line. So, answering your plea is already highly irregular. Then he started sending us up."

Phin paused and rubbed a hand over the back of his neck. It was an endearing gesture and almost had me telling him to forget it, but I couldn't. I needed to know.

"The three of us aren't what you would call top-tier demons. We're kind of misfits, for a variety of reasons. So being hand-picked by the demon lord was unexpected. After Jax and I got here, we realized there was no one assigned to you. At first, we assumed it was because he wanted your soul since you were the one who cast the spell and Asmodeus has a thing about witches, but we've kind of come to the conclusion he might just want you."

"Why the hell would he want me?" I honestly couldn't imagine what a demon lord would want with an aging white woman from the suburbs. Sure, I was pretty enough, but not exactly beautiful. I was smart, but not a genius. I was perfectly average, to be honest.

"I don't know, Vi." Phin offered me a soft smile. It was still slightly menacing with his sharp teeth. "All I know is I've been a demon for a few hundred years and I've never seen him behave this way. There's a reason he's here, and it looks like the reason is you."

We sat in silence as I thought about that. About the implications of Phin's words. I shredded my muffin into crumbs as I tried to figure out what about me would draw a high-ranking demon to Earth. I was no saint, but I never thought I would be going to Hell based on my actions. Until that silly, drunken night nearly a year ago, I'd never so much as considered magic or demons as real. There was nothing about me interesting enough to catch the attention of a demon lord.

"I don't know, Vi. Be careful. Asmodeus isn't the worst demon in Hell, but he's still a very powerful demon lord. I wouldn't want to cross him." Phin rested his hand on my shoulder and squeezed. The gesture was friendly, but there was a warning there too. He was worried. I could feel the knot in my stomach tightening.

This was bad.

This was very, very bad.

Chapter Five

There were lights on in my house. Light blazed from half of the windows in my little two-story cottage. The demon was still there.

I briefly wondered if I could get someone to perform an exorcism, but the interactions I'd had with the church discussing demons had not been very positive. So, I would not hold my breath if any of them would be able, or willing, to help me.

I climbed out of my car and walked the short path up to my door. I stood outside, trying to drop my shoulders and unclench my jaw. Going in fighting wouldn't be productive, and I wanted this demon gone.

As calm as I could be, I unlocked and opened my front door. Immediately my calm left me. There were strangers in my house. Not only strangers, but strange-looking creatures. They seemed to be everywhere.

I was used to seeing Candy, Phin, and Jax in their demon forms. They were beautiful in an oddly terrifying way. But very humanoid. These creatures seemed to be made of little more than shadows and had more limbs than a being should have. Multi-tentacled legs met torsos with too many arms. There were at least three of them in my space.

They didn't react to me as I slammed my door and stormed through the house to the dining room, where I found Asmodeus still in werewolf form sprawled out at my table. The small rectangular table was covered in papers, two laptops, and a tablet. Standing beside him was a distinctly female demon. She was a dark purple with long lavender hair and her tiny black dress was more strategically placed fabric, than an actual garment. She leaned over the table with her boobs nearly in Asmodeus' face as she asked him to sign something. She was the first to look up when I came in, and the smile she gave me was downright evil. It was the kind of smile I'd take offense to, if I had or wanted any claim on the man in question.

"Your toy is here." She said in a smoky, sexy voice. She placed a hand on Asmodeus' shoulder as she said it. The possessive move actually made me want to laugh.

"Violet, so glad you're back." Completely ignoring the demon, he shoved his chair back and rounded the table to greet me. A concerningly large, petty part of me wanted to give the demon a smug look at her total dismissal. But I really didn't want to give the impression I was interested in the beast.

A beast who now towered over me. His dark eyes glowed with an inner light as he stared down at me.

"It's my house." I said, propping my hands on my hips. I refused to let him think he was intimidating me. Even though a part of me kind of expected him to end whatever game, this was and rip my soul from my body.

I wondered if it hurt? Like, does your soul still feel pain after it's left the skin suit, where all the pain receptors are? It'd have to, right? Otherwise, what was the point of punishment in Hell?

"Yes. It's very quaint." He looked around without any real interest before looking back at me. "I assure you; you'll find our palace comfortable."

Our palace? OUR PALACE?

Nope.

I was not going to take that one on.

I spun away from him and headed into the kitchen to throw a bag of frozen veggies and pasta in the microwave for dinner. I was hungry. I was tired. I was not dealing with a delusional demon and his petty secretary, girlfriend, desk pet.

"Assuming, pushy, invasive asshole." I muttered to myself as I pulled the bag of pasta out of the freezer and started pulling the end open to create a vent.

"Invading assholes wasn't on my list of things

to do today, but I could be persuaded." A voice growled from behind me.

I screamed and jumped, ripping the end of the bag wide open and sending my dinner flying into the air and watching in horror as it landed on my clean counters and floors. I whirled around to glare at the demon behind me.

"Why won't you just leave me alone?" I yelled at him.

"I have no desire to." He was leaning against the door frame, his arms crossed against his broad, black chest.

"Do you have a desire to get stabbed? Because you're very close to getting stabbed." The knife block was on the other side of the kitchen. There was no way I'd get to it in time before he stopped me. But it was a nice fantasy, for a moment.

"Possibly. It's not my kink, but I'm down for trying anything once." His long pink tongue swept out along his sharp teeth, his eyes banked flames. The psycho was actually getting turned on by this.

I scoffed. "As if."

It was an admittedly lame response, but I had nothing in the face of being told I could stab someone and they might like it. I mean, where do you even go from there?

Instead of waiting for his response, I headed to the pantry for my broom to sweep up my dinner. Goddamn it, I was starving.

"So, stabbing is off the table. I'll make a note of it." The laughter in his voice kind of made me wish I could put it back on the table. But I was probably too squeamish to actually stab him, anyway. I wasn't a big fan of blood.

There was a snap behind me and suddenly one of the shadow creatures was beside me, reaching for the broom. I yelped and dropped it. The thing easily caught it and went to work cleaning up my mess.

"I apologize for your dinner. Will you let me feed you?" Asmodeus was close when I turned around, and I wondered how he'd crossed the tiled floor of my kitchen on claws without making a sound.

His clawed hand reached for my hair and I stepped back as far as I could, finding myself trapped between him and the cabinets, the counter digging into my back.

"No. I'll let you take your demons and your stuff and get out of my house and out of my life."

"But you summoned me, love. You wanted me in your life." He leaned close, his muzzle going into my hair at my neck. "You called to me. And here I am. Things will be so much better once you stop fighting it."

His breath was warm on my neck and when his tongue swept across my skin the sensation that shuddered through my body was not revulsion. I closed that thought down quickly and shoved him back. He went slowly, trailing his furry jaw against mine as he moved.

"I am pretty sure I was trying to call to the goddess, not the devil."

"And yet, I'm the one who heard your plea." His hand came up again, claws tangled in my hair to angle my head back. It wasn't painful or rough, but I didn't want to be trapped by him. "The universe is quirky sometimes."

"The universe can bite me." I said, glaring up at him as I tried to keep my breath even.

The beast laughed, a booming sound I could feel rattle through me. "It's not interested. But I am. You'd better believe I will."

He released me, stepping backward and out of my space. Taking advantage of the distance, I ducked around him and left the room. I was tired of running in my own house, but I was more scared of what I would do if I stayed.

Chapter Six

I spent the rest of the night hiding in my room, hating myself for allowing the demon to take over my house. I didn't know how to get rid of it. I'd called and asked Fern if I could try an exorcism, but Jax said that would probably only make him itchy and very mad.

I flipped through the book of spells we'd used to see if there was anything in there, but I already knew there wasn't. There was not a single mention of a demon of any kind in the book. It made me wonder for the millionth time how and why we'd been entangled in this mess with Asmodeus. It really did not make sense.

The next morning, I woke alone. I changed quickly and snuck out of the house without looking for the demon werewolf. There were still hours until I was supposed to be taking the little girl I was nannying for the summer to a birthday party at the local skating rink, so I went to a local coffee shop for a hit of caffeine and a breakfast sandwich. While I sat there waiting, I used my phone to search for ways to get protection against demons. I had a feeling it was all a bunch of nonsense, but I was totally going to get some salt and try putting some protection symbols on my bedroom door.

Couldn't hurt, right?

Just before noon, I headed across town to the skating rink. Normally I was firm on not working weekends, but Logan was a full-time single dad and had a work event. His daughter was pretty much impossible to say no to. Which said a lot, because I was a teacher and spent all day every day telling little kids no.

A part of me wished there was any sort of spark with Logan. It could have been so easy to fall in love with someone like him. In fact, he checked so many of the boxes on my man bucket list, including being tall, blond, and good with kids. I had absolutely zero interest in having my own children, but I did love kids. Being a good parent was usually a pretty good indicator of how someone would be with their romantic partner.

I wasn't halfway down the walk to the door before a high-pitched voice yelled my name. Moments later I was bowled over by a pixie of a girl with lots of straight golden hair and wide, blue eyes. Lily was five, three years younger than the third graders I taught during the school year. She had been in Fern's class last year, and had introduced me to Logan when he'd asked her about possible summer care options. Fern was teaching summer school, but I had planned to take the summer off. For Fern's sake, I'd taken the meeting with Logan, fully prepared to let him down easy. But I'd fallen in love with the ball of energy who was Lily.

"Hi there," I said, kneeling to give the little girl a big hug and throwing a grin to Logan over her shoulder. "Are you excited to go skating?"

"So, so 'cited!" She said, spinning out of my arms and doing a turn to show off the purple tutu-dress she was wearing. It was very over the top for a roller rink, but Lily was firmly in her princess era. It was next to impossible to get her into any-thing but a pretty dress. The poofier or glitterier the better.

"Thank you for doing this," Logan said. When I stood up and tugged on the slightly too short hem of my t-shirt.

I hadn't been able to do laundry and was run-ning short on clothing. Especially since I had been refusing to replace my wardrobe after gaining thirty-five pounds over the last year. I'd never believed in stress weight, but damn, it came at me with a vengeance.

I smiled up at the man and accepted the back-pack and gift bag he was handing out to me. "It's no problem. I'm happy to be out of the house to-day. You said you'd be back by three to get her?"

I didn't have a car seat in my car since every-thing we wanted to do was within walking dis-tance. If we did want to take an adventure further away, I would get the car seat from Logan before he left for the day.

"Yep. If I can get away sooner, I will. But I made it clear I had to be back here by three. I don't want to take up any more of your day than we already are." He ruffled a hand in the hair at the back of his head in a super endearing gesture. Once again, I wished I felt something, anything, for him. But there was nothing.

Just like there hadn't been any real sparks with anyone for well over a year.

The lack of spark had driven me to cast the spell in the first place. My parents had been harping on me about being single, going into my thirties and wanting grandkids. They kept going on and on about wanting to make sure I settled down and before they died. Which was ridiculous because they were both very healthy, active people in their mid-fifties. But I'd been depressed and lonely and was willing to try anything to get them to back off. Even the occult, apparently.

And that worked out so well for me.

"It's my pleasure." I hiked the backpack over the shoulder opposite of my tote bag and looped the gift bag over my wrist. "Are you ready to rock, Lil?"

"Yep!" She threw herself against her dad's legs. Experienced with her fierce tackle hugs, he already braced for impact. "Bye Dad!"

I took Lily's hand in mine and we went our separate ways.

"C'mon Violet!" Lily said, pulling on my

hand. "I'm so 'cited! I've never been roller skating before."

"Yep, let's go skate." I allowed her to drag me into the building, thankful to finally have something to focus on besides my demon problem.

Chapter Seven

"Are you sure you don't want to go to the hospital? You shouldn't take chances with head wounds." Logan reached up to touch the lump and growing bruise on my face, but stopped short and returned his hand to the gear shift between us.

"I'm sure. It's just a bump. I'll be fine." I turned to smile at Lily in the back seat. "Are you okay now?"

The little girl nodded; her face still buried in her teddy bear's neck. The bob of her pigtails was really the only indication she'd heard me. I wanted to soothe her again, but my face was throbbing and my head started to hurt. Her father would make sure she knew I wasn't angry, and she wasn't in trouble.

"If you start feeling sick or getting dizzy–"

"I'll have someone take me to the emergency room. But it'll be fine." I could tell by his expression he didn't believe me, and didn't want to leave me alone in my house with a head injury. "Don't worry, I have a friend staying with me at the moment. They'll make sure I'm taken care of."

There was no telling what the demon's version of care would look like. And it would amuse him to no end, knowing I'd called that beast my friend.

"Well, that makes me feel better." I pushed open my door and grabbed my bag from the floor by my feet. "Take care of yourself. And go ahead and take Monday off. I've got some vacation time. I don't want you pushing yourself too hard."

"You really don't have to." I'd been planning on being with Lily to avoid the beast and his hoard of demons who had taken over my house.

"I really do." His hand came up to brush my hair back and gently probe the lump over my eye. It was a sweet, gentle move that briefly had my stomach clenching. But even with my body physically reacting to his touch, I simply wasn't attracted to him. "I'm so sorry this happened."

"I'm sorry too," came a small voice from the back seat. It was filled with tears and I wished I could make her believe it really was okay.

"It was an accident. No one was to blame." Honestly, if anyone was to blame, it was me. I had no business being on roller skates. "Are you sure you're okay to get my car back to me?"

Logan nodded and pointed to my car keys in the cup holder between us. "I'll get someone to help me drive it over here. It's the least we can do. Now go take care of yourself. I'll check in later."

I nodded and got out of the car, closing the door behind me. Logan sat idling at the curb as I walked the short path to my front door and got the key in the lock. I waved him off as I headed into the house.

Dropping my bag and house keys on the floor beside the door, I headed to the kitchen and the ice pack I knew was somewhere in my freezer. My face was throbbing. I hadn't looked at it since we left the skating rink thirty minutes before, but I could feel the skin getting tight and just knew I was going to have a hell of a bruise.

"What the fuck?" Asmodeus said from behind me. My body was heavy as I slowly turned around, holding the ice pack to the lump above my right eye. "You're hurt."

"Powerful observation skills." I said dryly, too tired to get into it with him. From the growl in his voice and the agitation in his stance, fighting is exactly what he had in mind. Leaning back against the counter, I held my ground as he stalked across the room to me.

"Who did this to you?" Asmodeus' voice was a deep rumble I could feel in my chest. He reached a hand up to brush against the bruise on my face, the touch gentle on my skin. "Tell me who hurt you."

"No one." I brushed his hand away from my head. I didn't want him to be nice to me. The part of me that loved reading dark romance loved being on the receiving end of a good "who hurt you," I didn't want it from Asmodeus. I wanted nothing from him.

"Violet," his voice somehow, impossibly, got lower. "I'll have their name."

"Well, I don't stop to ask the name of the pole I slammed my face into." I prodded the growing lump and winced. As much from the embarrassment of falling face first into the handrail, as I was from the pain. I was counting down until I could take another dose of painkiller.

"Oh love, I'm as old as time. Do you think I haven't heard every excuse in the book?" He grabbed my upper arms, his claws digging into my flesh. He brought his face close to mine and growled. Actually fucking growled at me. "Now tell me who did this."

"It was an accident." I gritted out at him. "Now take your damn hands off of me before you're the one to put bruises on me."

His claws immediately released me, and he clasped them behind his back. I rubbed my arms where he had gripped me. It hadn't been hard enough to break the skin, but I could still feel the weight and heat of his paws.

I gentled my tone, trying to be the voice of reason, since Asmodeus clearly wasn't reasonable.

"Look, I'm clumsy as fuck. And had no business being on roller skates. The little girl I was nannying lost her balance, knocked me over into a pole. There are about three dozen witnesses, to my shame, that will confirm no one laid a hand on me. It's fine. Let it go."

I rubbed a hand up and down his arm before reclaiming my ice pack off of the counter and heading out of the room. I'd made it a couple of steps before he grabbed my arm.

The move was gentle. I could have shaken him off at any point. Which was the only reason I stopped.

"I don't like seeing marks on you. Especially not your face." He brought his hand up to cup my cheek, claws sinking gently into my hair. "You are so lovely."

I snorted, knowing full-well it was a line. I was short, about a hundred pounds overweight, and average-looking in every way. The single thing interesting about me was my hair, currently pink, and likely to change color again before the month was out. I wasn't Quasimodo or anything, but I wasn't someone who was ever going to stop traffic.

Asmodeus moved to stand in front of me. Both hands came up to cradle my face. "Do not dismiss me. I may be a demon, but I will not lie to you. From the moment I heard your call, I knew you would be mine. Your soul is a flame and I am but a moth."

"I'm not yours." I stepped back, shaking myself free from his grasp. My hands were shaking and my stomach was jittery, but I would not fall for his lines. "I don't want anything from you."

Chapter Eight

Asmodeus drew himself up and stalked toward me. I backed away, not wanting to take my eyes off of the annoyed demon. My heart was racing but stuttered nearly to a stop when my back hit the wall and I found myself trapped.

His arms came up, hands resting on the wall on either side of my head. I was trapped in the cage of his body. I shuddered, heat and chill raced through my body at once.

"There is nothing I wouldn't do for you," the demon growled. "You are mine."

Heat shot through me at the words, quick and unwanted. This demon held the fate of my soul in his hands. It may literally be his, but the rest of me didn't have to be. Despite, what my traitorous body seemed to be thinking.

"Just because everyone in Hell is ready to lick your ass, doesn't mean I'm about to bow before you." I shoved back against his chest. As usual, it didn't work. The beast didn't move a millimeter.

"You have such interesting and unexpected kinks. First knife play and now you're into ass licking. I never would have taken you for such a deviant." He ran his tongue up my neck to breathe warmly on my ear.

I shuddered.

"I like your claws, love. Feel free to dig them in whenever, and wherever, you like."

Deciding to take him literally, I brought my hands up to his wrists and dug my nails into the hair-covered flesh. His teeth scraped against my neck and I released him, worried I'd gone too far and this was the moment he ripped my throat out.

He used his muzzle to shove my head back and latch his teeth around my neck. It was a threat, a warning. But when his tongue came out to lick the column of my throat, I couldn't help the jolt that shot through my body, warming me from neck to pussy.

There was something very, very wrong with me. I absolutely should not get turned on by this beast and his teeth on my throat. He let out a low growl and released me. "I can smell you, love. I can smell your sweet cunt getting wet for me. Deny it all you want, but your body knows who it belongs to."

This time, when I dug my nails into his wrists, I didn't hold back. He hissed in pain and pulled away from me.

"Little witch." He growled at me. But I was too angry to be afraid. Angry at him and angry at myself.

"I don't belong to you." I said, sliding out from between him and the wall. "Leave me the fuck alone."

I grabbed the ice pack I'd dropped at some point during the encounter and stormed up the stairs to my room.

I locked the door, knowing it would do nothing to keep him out if he really wanted in. But it made me feel better.

Crawling into bed, I laid down and plopped the ice pack on my face and tried to ignore the heat and slickness between my legs.

The demon owned my soul, but he would not have my body, I told myself again. This time, I was afraid it was a lie.

Chapter Nine

My skin felt too tight, and fire banked inside my pussy. I needed an orgasm, and I needed it now.

The demon was somewhere in the house out there and the flimsy knob lock wouldn't keep him out if he really wanted in. But I really needed to come.

I kicked the blankets off the bed and tore my clothing from my body. Fuck the foreplay, I thought, as I dropped a hand between my legs to firmly circle around my clit. I tried to picture the dream that woke me so hot and horny, but I couldn't remember the details. I remembered the feeling of being full and stretched. Now I ached with how empty I felt.

I circled my clit in quickening movements. Panting, I fought to maintain my breathing as pleasure wound through me. My cream leaked from my pussy as I drew closer and closer to orgasm.

The door flew open, banging into the wall and causing me to jump. Asmodeus stood in the doorway. His breath burst from him like a bellows, as his eyes took me in. I'd nearly jumped out of my skin when the door opened and was now laying splayed against the bed. His nostrils flared as I dropped my hands over my pussy to cover myself.

"Get out!" I yelled at him, stomach clenching as the orgasm I'd been so close to dissipated. The blanket was on the floor, but the sheet was within range. I reached for it only for Asmodeus to launch himself forward to snag the fabric before I could. He flung it across the room and I shouted at him.

"Do you have any idea what you're doing to me right now?" His voice was gravel, growling through my whole body. He grabbed my ankle and tugged me toward him. I yelped and reached for the pillow to cover myself. He snatched it away too.

"Do you have any idea what the smell of you is doing to me?" He dropped to his haunches and leaned forward, taking the scent of me in.

I flushed hot, both embarrassed for being so exposed and turned on by his intensity and touch. He adjusted his grip, pulling me to the edge of the bed.

"I can feel your pleasure, and it is shuddering through me like my own. I need to taste you." He drew my other leg toward him, opening me. My hands still covered my cunt, but my resolve was wavering as the heat of his breath blew over my throbbing flesh.

"Tell me, no." He said, as he licked a path up my knee to mid-thigh. His paws came to rest on my knees, opening my legs wide to fit him. I should have fought him. I didn't want him or what he had to offer. Hadn't I sworn he wouldn't get my body? But as he licked another stripe up my leg, I wanted to give into him.

"Tell me to stop. Tell me to leave and I will." Another slow, hot lick up my inner thigh. "Otherwise, I'm going to eat this pretty, dripping pussy until you can't feel your legs. Then I'm going to make you come one more time just for my pleasure."

Everything froze. I stopped struggling against him. He crouched there between my splayed legs with claws wrapped around my thick thighs. His eyes were hot on me, fire burning in the darkness. But he didn't move, waiting for my answer.

This was where I was supposed to tell him to leave. He'd given me the power to stop everything, and I knew I should. But this was the first time in over a year someone had set me aflame. This was the first time in so long I wasn't the only one invested in my pleasure. Sure, he was the enemy and would take my life in a few short weeks, but why shouldn't I have this? Wasn't it more reason to allow myself to take what I wanted?

Hadn't I wondered since I was too young to admit what it would be like to have a werewolf eat me out? The demon had said he'd taken the form I'd chosen. Didn't that mean he wanted to give me this? That I wanted this all along?

I tangled a hand in his fur behind his pointed ear and tugged. "Shut the fuck up and do it already."

His growl shook the windows before he pressed a hand to my chest and forced me back. He pulled my legs impossibly wide and did as he was told.

The first swipe of his tongue from opening to clit was unexpected. His tongue was impossibly warm and firm. It didn't move slick against my soaked flesh like a human tongue might. Instead, it tugged the sensitive flesh, pulling against it, sending spikes of pleasure through me.

Before I could think of the sensation, he was doing it again. And again. Long, firm, licks over and over. His tongue was more like a dog's. Long, firm, and just a little rough as it lapped at my cunt like a starving man.

It might have reminded me of the first time I'd had a guy go down on me. Neither of us had a clue what we were doing. It was pretty much the same move as Asmodeus was doing.

But As' tongue was so long and thick it was almost like a burning, wet, textured dick was being rubbed between my folds. Which sounded terrible, but gods it felt anything but.

Heat built in me when he scraped his teeth over me before plunging his tongue into my hole. It wriggled its way in, forcing past the tension of unused muscles to move perfectly over some magical place that had me moaning out and seeing stars.

His answering growl had me arching off the bed and sinking my hand into his fur again. My legs were shaking where they pressed against Asmodeus' grip. Pleasure was so intense; my body didn't know what it wanted. My hips dipped away from him and fought his grip even while my hand in his fur pulled him closer, deeper.

My free hand moved to grasp my boob as his tongue plunged in and out of me, moving in waves inside of me and driving me insane. I tweaked my nipple and gasped. His eyes flicked to mine. Held.

He pulled out of me and before I even processed that, his tongue was flicking against my clit. The wide muscle wrapped around the whole thing and pulsed.

"Oh god, oh god, oh god." I panted. Pulling desperately on his hair while roughly twisting my nipple.

"There's no god here. There's only you and me." He bent back to work for a couple rough strokes of his tongue.

"If you're going to chant anyone's name while I'm inside you, it'll be mine."

"Shut up and make me come already." I growled at him, refusing to back down and give him what he wanted. This wasn't about him or us, it was about me.

My growl turned into a scream when As

moved and pulled me off the bed entirely. He held me so my legs still straddled his face. He turned us and lowered onto the bed. I was barely done with the first scream when I yelped again, as he flung himself back onto the bed and pulled me with him. I ended up straddling his neck.

"You want to come so bad, then do it." His claws grasped my ass, the flesh overflowing his wide grip. He yanked again, pulling me up over his head. "Take what you need, love."

The position was never one of my favorites. I was too big, and I was constantly worried about smothering the man with my pussy. Having to explain to emergency services lived rent free in my head. Plus, from below there wasn't much of a view besides my rounded belly and tits bouncing up and down. I could never get out of my head enough to enjoy it.

As didn't give me a chance to second guess anything. He moved one paw to press against my belly and began moving me. His tongue was out and firm against my pulsating flesh. It didn't take much for me to take over movement.

With Asmodeus' help, I moved against him. Grinding my dripping cunt against his muzzle and tongue. He shifted so he could thrust his tongue inside of me, getting so much deeper from that angle. His damp nose pressed against my clit.

I dug my hands into his shoulders and held on as I finally came.

I was still shaking from the force of the orgasm when we were moving again. Asmodeus flipped us, I was sprawled on my stomach, his tongue still buried between my legs. The sensitive flesh pulsed around him as he hauled my hips up and dove in deeper. His tongue was so wide. Certainly, wider than any guy I'd been with. The stretch as he reached deep, devouring me, was intense.

I wanted to tell him to stop. I wanted it to never end.

As let out a deep growl as my legs shook inside the hooks of his arms and I came again.

"You taste so fucking sweet." He licked a wide swipe up from my clit to my back hole. I jerked in his grasp, and he chuckled deeply against my skin. "You're better than I'd ever imagined you would be."

Another long, languid stroke of his tongue had me trying to jerk away. I wasn't into anal play and I definitely never had anyone go near it with their mouth. My body was confused by the sensation.

"Sweet." Lick.

"Succulent." Lick.

"Perfection." Lick.

"I could do this forever and never get enough." His tongue thrust into my starfish and I yelped, pulling away. But his grip wasn't letting me go anywhere.

He didn't go deep or hard, but he pressed firmly, stretching my flesh wide around his massive tongue. Shifting positions, he brought one arm around my belly, securing me in place. His other paw went between my legs where he used the back of his knuckles to grind into my clit as he tasted me.

"Mine." he growled, circling his tongue around my tight hole. "You belong to me."

"I don't belong to anyone."

It probably would have sounded more convincing if I hadn't been panting and moaning at the time. But the point apparently got across because the next thing I knew, Asmodeus was growling and shoving his tongue deep, deep inside of me. The knuckle that had been gently rubbing me pressed down and picked up pace, to match the rapid movements of his tongue in and out and around my aching flesh.

The hand between my legs turned and his claw was now rubbing against one of my favorite parts of my anatomy. I arched my body so I could watch as the sharp point teased my nub. It bordered on pain and, mixed with the building pleasure, was enough to send me over the edge for the third time.

My body collapsed onto the bed. I couldn't feel my legs and I didn't much care. I laid there panting as wet paws withdrew from my body.

"There's a good girl, my love. Now you'll give me one more." I let out a weak laugh. There was no way. I was spent. Gone. Done.

The laugh turned into a yelp as I was flipped over to lay on my back. As crawled up my body, licking and nipping at my skin.

He used his paws to spread my thighs wide and settled his body between them. I could feel his cock pressed between us. He slicked it through my heat and I shuddered. He was so, so large.

"I'm not going to fuck you," he said, gliding his giant dick between my lips, across my over-stimulated clit. His breathing kicked up as he growled into my ear. "I'm going to get my dick nice and lubed up until you come. But I'm not going to fuck you until you beg me for it."

I was about ready to beg for it. I'd had three orgasms and my pussy was clenching on nothing and it was an almost painful ache. I needed more. I needed him in me.

"I can see you thinking about it." He thrust forward and circled his hips. Focusing his attention on my clit. "I won't do it. I want you to want me when you're not out of your mind with pleasure. I know I could have you right now with one thrust."

He moved his hips and was suddenly there, at my entrance. So hard and hot. I arched up against him, but he moved away with a chuckle. "Oh, my needy little slut, I could have you. But it doesn't count right now."

I whined, needing to be filled. I gripped his furry shoulders and ground back against him.

"Please As, I need more."

His chuckle was gravel. His breath was the bellows. He moved over me with slick movements that made obscene noises as my cream coated both of us.

"Take what you need, love." We rolled again, and he was under me. I rose up and used my hands on his chest to brace me as I rode him. I could have taken him. The need to have him inside me was so great, but I ground against him. He wasn't budging, and I wasn't taking what he wasn't offering. No matter how much we both wanted it.

Asmodeus' claws came to my hips, helping move me back and forth. Holding me against him. I looked down and jerked in his grasp.

I'd never considered what a werewolf cock would actually look like, but it was definitely not like a human dick. It was thick and veiny. The dark red color looked painful and angry. The head wasn't a full mushroom cap but more angled, with a flared head on one side.

And it was huge.

I wouldn't compare it to my forearm. But it wasn't far off. Like, maybe the forearm of a skinny person. Either way, the thing was huge.

The most notable thing though, was the large round knot at the base of his cock. It was half again the circumference of his shaft and I shuddered as I imagined the stretch of it inside me.

"That's right, love. Think about how good it would be." He circled his hips and brought me down against him.

"Look at you, splayed around me and so wet."

Thrust.

"Listen to how soaked you are."

Thrust.

"I can't stop thinking about how good you taste."

Thrust. Thrust. Thrust.

"I'm going to love making you mine."

He jerked me hard against him, and I exploded. My hands fisted in the fur on his chest and my legs shook. I felt weak and lightheaded as I crashed down against him.

I shoved up as the first spurt of cum hit my belly. It was hot, like dipping a finger in a cooling candle wax. It didn't burn. Not exactly. More of the heat of a fresh sunburn.

"Look what you made me do." He grumbled, reaching between us to grab his cock and stroke it. A few more spurts sprayed out, splattering my belly and his. He groaned before taking my hand and sliding it through the sticky fluid on my belly. He brought it to my lips.

With only a moment of hesitation, I opened my mouth and allowed him to push my fingers between my lips. It wasn't something I'd usually do, but there was a part of me curious to know what the demon tasted like. The answer was spicy, like cloves and cinnamon.

"I'd prefer if it was my cock you were sucking my cum off of, but watching you do it is nearly as good. Someday." I removed my fingers from my mouth and rolled off of him. I laid sprawled on my back, staring at the ceiling.

What the fuck had I just done?

"There isn't going to be a someday." I said quietly.

"Yes, there will." He was so sure, and that confidence struck my anger like flint to moss.

"No, there won't be. This was a mistake. Everything about you being here has been a mistake." I got up and grabbed a baggy shirt out of my dresser and yanked it on. With all the weight I'd gained recently, it barely covered my ass but it was better than being naked.

He surged off of the bed and stalked me down. I stood my ground, refusing to cower before him. I'm not sure at what point I stopped being afraid of him, but I was fairly certain he wasn't going to hurt me.

"Nothing about us is a mistake." He reached out and tangled a hand in my hair. "One day, you'll see that."

He released me and walked out of my room. If it felt colder without his presence, I ignored it.

Chapter Ten

"You lying, conniving, manipulative piece of shit!" I stormed into the dining room Asmodeus had turned into an office. He was sitting at the table with the femme fatale demon standing beside him again. She let out an exaggerated gasp. We both ignored her as the demon lord gave me a wide smile that was absolutely terrifying in the werewolf form.

I was too angry to be scared.

"You made this morning happen. You manipulated me and then pretended to be the good guy. You are the lowest type of scum." I'd picked up a vase I'd bought from the dollar store years ago and threw it at him. He dodged but there was some satisfaction in the crash it made against the wall.

"You dare attack our lord?" The female demon gasped.

"Damn fucking right I dare." I picked up a coffee mug left on the side table and threw it. He deflected it and it smashed into the demon assistant's stomach. Good.

"What is it you're accusing me of, my love?" He shoved back from the table, ignoring the injured demon beside him.

"I'm not your love." I ground out. When he was within touching distance, I grabbed his wrist and tugged him out of the room and away from his demon assistant.

"You're my queen and one day I'll take you to our palace and worship you in all the ways you deserve." He nipped at my shoulder when I came to a stop. I released him and stepped away, ignoring the flash of heat that went through me.

I spun to face him. My hands on my hips and my glare firmly on his lying face. Anger blazed through me so hot I was surprised I hadn't burst into flames.

How had it taken me so long to realize the demon lord of all sex demons had manipulated his way into my bed? Clover had told us about how Candy had invaded her dreams while still in her stuffed candy corn form. Clover said it was some of the best sex she's ever had, and she woke up the horniest she'd ever felt in her life.

Just like I'd woken up that morning. When he'd been so conveniently there to help me out.

"You fucked me in my dream so I would fuck you in real life." I accused him. His eyes blazed heat and I fought not to step back. I wasn't going to cower before him. He already owned my soul.

What more could he take from me? I had nothing more to fear from him.

"Dreaming of me, love?" His voice was dangerously low. He slid the back of his claws down the column of my neck and I fought back a shudder at the gentle touch and implied threat. "How sweet."

"There was nothing sweet about it. You manipulated me!" I poked a finger into his chest, drilling the digit through the fur and into the muscle. "You took advantage."

He grabbed my hand and wrapped it behind my back, pulling me into and against him. "I didn't take anything not offered. I gave you the option to stop me. I told you to stop me."

I struggled against his grip, squirming against his body. It was a mistake. My nipples came to attention and my breathing sped up. I could feel Asmodeus growing hard between us.

"Anything you dreamed was on you. I have not, and will not meddle in your head. When I claim you, it will be because you've chosen me."

"I'll never choose you." I spat, jerking against him.

Those claws on my neck again, curling around it. I stilled, not wanting to tempt fate, or the devil, and have my throat ripped out. My pulse pounded through my body, a dangerous mix of fear and lust. When I squirmed against his body, it had nothing to do with escape.

"Oh, fuck it." One moment I was pinned against a seven-foot furry werewolf. The next moment I was pressed against a nearly as tall demon. I barely had a chance to glance before I was pulled impossibly closer and his mouth crashed down on mine. I had an impression of black and red but then I was lost to the kiss.

It was angry and demanding. His tongue forced its way past my lips to tangle with mine. Teeth sank into my lip and I yelped. My free arm went up to curl around the back of his neck, buried under black curls. I yanked him down toward me, pressing us impossibly tighter.

What the hell are you doing, girl? The sane part of my brain yelled at me. But I was too far gone. I ignored the voice of sanity and sank into the moment.

His hand released my arm. Both slid down my sides, and over my hips to cup my ass. As was bent in half to reach me as he hauled me off my feet and up against his hard torso. I yelped.

"Too heavy." I gasped, pushing against his shoulders.

"I'm a demon, love." Human-like teeth sank into my neck. "I can do things your mortal lovers couldn't even imagine."

He lowered me to grind my pussy against his bare, rigid cock. I whined and moved against him. My pants and underwear were in the way of me getting what my aching cunt needed.

"You may not want me, yet, but you're a little slut for my cock and what I can do to you." Asmodeus said, sliding me against him until the seam of my leggings were damp in my cream and his pre-cum. My insides quivered.

"It's okay," He changed his grip on me and the next thing I knew, he was driving his claws through my clothing until they brushed against overly-sensitive skin. The sound of rending cotton filled the air as he shredded my leggings.

"Holy shit." I muttered, pressing my soaked cunt against his cock. I leaned back, trusting him to hold me, and looked down between our bodies.

He was lean and muscular and I wanted to lick the little dips that framed his hips. His cock was the same as when he was in werewolf form. So red, thick, and veiny. It was fascinating and beautiful.

And I wanted it inside me.

I shifted, trying to line my aching hole up to him, but he lifted me up so I was straddling his torso.

"Oh no, my love. I told you; I'm not fucking you until you're mine." He shifted his grip and hauled me further up his body. "Don't worry, I'll give you what you need."

I screamed as he lifted me to straddle his face. I had to bend over and grasp his horns to prevent myself from hitting my head on the ceiling or falling off.

Before I was perfectly settled, his mouth was there.

His tongue was a hot brand against my innermost flesh. It was different than when he'd done this as a werewolf, but still more than any human man had ever done. He went deeper, his tongue wider. It spread me enough to have me clenching against him. I slammed one hand against the ceiling, gripping his black ram-like horns with the other hand and held on for dear life as he ate me like a starving man having his last meal.

The position was far from comfortable, but after a few moments I stopped worrying about falling from seven feet in the air and gave myself over to the feeling. This was a position I didn't believe was possible and definitely never expected to find myself in at nearly two-hundred and thirty pounds. But there I was, riding his face with firm hands locking me in place.

I gripped the base of his horns, and he groaned into me. The sensation was enough to have me gushing on his face. I took it to mean his horns were sensitive and gripped harder, stroking one of them while I used the other to hold myself up.

As licked, and fucked, and sucked me until I was squirming. All the while, I kept up my erratic strokes of his horns. They were jet black and bone smooth until the bottom where they connected to his head, where it seemed to be the most sensitive. There it was rough, hard, and bumpy. I gently circled it with my finger, which made him buck. I stopped, afraid he would drop me.

I tucked the information away for later. Not that I wanted there to be a later, but the effect he had on me was like nothing I'd ever experienced before. When he touched me, I couldn't say no. I didn't want to. He made me feel wanted in a way I'd never experienced before.

It was heady and all-consuming. And when he sucked my clit into his mouth, hard and deep, I exploded. I'd always assumed the term "Seeing fireworks" was bullshit, but there was a whole galaxy bursting behind my eyes.

As worked me through my orgasm, gently pressing on until I slumped over his head. I had to be suffocating him, but I was too spent to move. After a moment, he helped me lower down to the floor. But he didn't release me. Instead, he held me tight against him. For a moment, I let myself feel treasured, wanted, valued.

"You are so beautiful." He muttered into my hair, rubbing a hand gently up and down my back.

For a moment, I let myself believe it.

Chapter Eleven

"Will you let me feed you?" Asmodeus asked me as he led me, mostly-naked, into the dining room. My leggings were a lost cause. As had decided my shirt was in the way and had fought it off me while I was taking my destroyed leggings off. The room was empty, his slutty secretary nowhere in sight.

"Why do you keep wanting to feed me? Is this some Hades/Persephone shit where it will bind me to you for eternity?" I didn't mention the fact he already owned my soul.

"No, it's because you're hungry and I don't like it. You don't eat enough." I scoffed, looking down at my round belly and thick thighs.

I didn't hate the way I looked, not really. I resented the extra weight I put on while stressing about this damn demon deal. And there I was, naked, about to have lunch with the same demon determined to steal my soul and claim me as his.

"You are a queen. I will happily worship you like one." He bent down and nipped at my neck, sharp fangs pressing against my skin. "But you need fuel or you'll pass out and what good would that do either of us?"

He had a point. I'd eaten a pathetically small amount since he'd arrived and after all of our acrobatics, I was drained and dehydrated. So, I allowed him to lead me into the kitchen and prop me on a counter with a glass of water while he made grilled cheese and ham sandwiches.

He was stunning in his demon form. He was the typical red devil without the cloven hooves. I wondered if Lucifer had them and then decided it was probably best not to ask. His skin was deep red, his horns and the tip of his flared tail were as black as his eyes. When he flashed me a grin, I could see the pointed edges to all of his teeth. Not just fangs.

Asmodeus was also built like a wet dream. Eight clearly defined abs, tall and muscular but not body builder bulky. I kind of wanted to take a bite out of his ass.

The thing I couldn't help but notice, as he moved around completely naked and clearly comfortable in the state, was the fact his dick remained the same as it had looked in his wolf form. Maybe not quite as big, but still the angry dark red with the odd flair around half the head.

"Is that your real cock?" I couldn't help but ask. And then slapped a hand over my mouth because what the hell type of question was that?

Thankfully, As laughed at my insane question instead of getting offended. "I'm a shapeshifter. My cock can take many forms but you seemed to like this one." He reached down and gave his flaccid peen a stroke, bringing it partially to attention. "But yes, the general appearance is what I'd call my own."

I watched as he circled the head with his thumb, pushing the flared edge back. A drop of pre-cum appeared, and he swiped it up with his thumb before bringing it to my mouth. I let him slide past my lips before licking the pad of his thumb. He shifted his hand to cup my face while his thumb remained in my mouth.

"Such a good little slut." I wasn't into degradation or being called names. If anything, I would have said I had a praise kink. But there was reverence in the way he said it made my whole body react.

He pulled back and returned to the stove, leaving me to wonder at my response to him. A part of me hated everything he stood for, for taking away my freedom and my choices. But when he touched me, and sometimes with the way he looked at me, it was like everything in me came alive in a way it had never been before. It was the thing missing from every relationship I'd been in and it was fundamentally unfair a demon gave it to me.

Lunch was an awkwardly naked affair. The conversation and company were fine. I wasn't used to hanging out in nothing but a bra and definitely not with other people. But Asmodeus refused to let me put my clothes back on. Going so far as to pin me in his lap when I tried. Which made eating more difficult, as I was painfully aware of his erection under me and his hands on my body.

His touch wasn't sexual. He wasn't groping me, but I couldn't help but be aware of his large hand on my stomach where he held me against him.

It wasn't an elegant position he had me in, straddling his leg, his arm wrapped under my boobs and keeping my back pressed against his front. His cock was half hard below my thigh. I kept fighting the urge to shift and rub my leg against him. I wanted to drive him as crazy as he had been driving me.

"Eat," Asmodeus demanded. He grasped my wrist and lifted the hand holding my sandwich to my mouth. I took the bite he demanded, but followed it up with wriggling on his lap, brushing my thigh against his cock.

The move backfired when my overly sensitive cunt and clit ground against the firm muscles in his leg. I gasped and As purred behind me.

He released his grasp on my wrist and slid his hand down my side to grasp my hip.

"Is my little kitten hungry for something else?" With his grip around my waist and on my hip, I was stuck just where he had me. Which was spread and exposed around his leg. He lifted his heel and brought the limb into firmer contact with my pussy. Using his grip on me, he slid me away and back again.

"No." I said, gripping the arm around my waist. "I'm fine with the sandwich, thank you."

I popped the last bite into my mouth and aggressively chewed, hoping to make a point.

He didn't take it.

Instead, he shifted his leg again, making contact with every bit of my exposed clit.

"Oh," he said, slipping a hand up over my hip and between my legs to toy with my clit. "Should I stop then?"

"No!" I was already on edge and a little angry he was able to get me there with so little effort.

"I didn't think so." Both hands moved to my thighs. My hips bucked, chasing his touch. "Take what you want, love. Ride my thigh like the little slut you are."

My pussy clenched, and I thought about telling him to let me go. I was sure he would if I said the words. But I didn't want him to let me go. I wanted to chase the feeling.

His breath was hot on my neck as his hands slid up my thighs to land on my hips.

"Ride me." It was an order and a plea.

I could feel his cock hard under my leg and I knew he hadn't come the last time in the living room. He had to be hard up by now.

I reached down and wrapped my hand around his cock. It was large, so large my fingers didn't quite reach around him. He was at least three hands long and I wondered if something so big could ever fit in me. I was no virgin, but that was a lot of peen.

With his cock hot in my hand, I began to move. I braced my other hand on his knee and rode his leg. I hadn't done something like this since middle school, and even then, it wasn't as filthy.

"Such a good little slut. So beautiful as you take your pleasure." A hand moved off of my hip and up over my ass. His fingers trailed down my spine, giving me the shivers. It was a sharp contrast to the heat coursing through my body.

"Touch me." I demanded, giving his dick a little squeeze. "Touch my tits."

The heavy weights were swaying back and forth with disturbing speed as I ground my cunt on his thigh. They were sore and sensitive and I was grateful when my torso was pulled back against the demon's body, as he reached around me to cup the globes. His hands were large, and I still overflowed them. He growled behind me before yanking down the cups so he could pinch and pull and tease my nipples.

"Do you hear that? Do you hear how wet your pretty, needy pussy is against my leg?" I slowed my breathing to see what he meant. He was right. The sound of my slick cunt filled the room as my most sensitive flesh ground against his thigh. I flushed red and hot. Oh gods, it was obscene.

He pinched my nipples hard and pulled. The pain yanked my focus from the sounds and my embarrassment. A small part of me hated he knew my body and mind so well already.

You know, the part of me that wasn't enjoying every moment of the pleasure he gave me.

His hand came down on my pussy in a light slap before he cupped my flesh and spread my lips wide.

"Who does this pussy belong to?" His voice echoed through me. I knew what he wanted, but I also knew I wasn't going to give him the satisfaction of the answer.

"It's attached to my body." I panted. The hand slapped my pussy again, and I jerked and jumped, but his grip on me kept me in place.

"There isn't a single part of you that doesn't belong to me." His fangs sank into my neck. Not enough to draw blood, but enough to send a flash of pain through me. "You are mine, Violet."

Oh, Hell no.

"Stop." I shoved at his hands and he released me. I pulled myself up off of his lap and spun around to glare at him. I crossed my arms over my breasts and fought the need to drop a hand to cover my cunt.

"Violet." His voice was a growl. His hand wrapped around his abandoned cock. I allowed myself a split second to process the sight before returning to glare at his stupid face.

"You don't get to sweep in here and claim me. I'm not yours. I'm not anyone's. No part of me belongs to you. Fuck, every time you seem even remotely redeemable you pull this shit." I waved both hands at him, at the table, at his cock. "Fuck off."

I didn't hear what he said as I stomped out of the room. It didn't matter. He didn't matter.

Chapter Twelve

Asmodeus left the house. I don't know how I knew it, but I was certain I could leave the bedroom and wouldn't see him.

It was dinnertime, which probably wasn't a coincidence. He'd made it clear he wanted me to eat. The defiant part of me wanted to skip dinner just to spite him. But I knew when I was cutting off my nose to spit in my face.

I was in the middle of my chicken and rice when the doorbell rang. Shocked the demon would show actual consideration, I flung the door open without looking through the peephole. The tall, blond man standing in the door surprised me.

"Logan?" I asked, confused.

"Hey, I brought your car back." He reached up and brushed a strand of hair out of my face and tucked it behind my ear. "How's the face?"

Honestly, in all of the events of the last twenty-four hours, I'd forgotten about my face. It was fine unless I touched it. Which I told Logan.

"Good, that's good. Lily still feels horrible about it." He dropped his hands into his pockets. I could see his car idling in the road behind him.

"She shouldn't. It was an accident. Better my face than hers." I rocked up to my toes and shoved my hands into my pants pocket as well. Gods, this felt awkward. And I didn't even know why.

"So, I know this is probably a terrible idea and crappy timing. I swear it has nothing to do with guilt about my daughter breaking your face but, uh, would you like to get dinner sometime? With me?"

I stood there, completely shocked. While Logan and I got along fine, I'd never put him into a dateable role. He'd never given me any reason to think I was anything but his daughter's nanny.

"I—"

"You are otherwise engaged." A voice from behind me said. I spun around to see Asmodeus in human form, a tall Icelandic god with cropped blond hair and sharp blue eyes that froze me with his look.

"Oh, I'm sorry, Violet. I didn't realize." Logan tugged my keys out of his pocket and held them out to me. "I'm going to head out. I'll see you tomorrow?"

"Oh, um, yeah. I'll be there." I watched him walk down the two steps to the pathway and then closed the door before slowly turning to face the demon behind me.

He was much closer than I'd expected. He

was also back in his werewolf form. The hulking black beast reached out and tangled a hand in my hair. It wasn't painful, but it was forceful as he tilted my head back to look me in the eye.

"Anything you want to talk about?" The calm purr didn't distract from the fire blazing in his gaze.

"How about you getting your fucking hands off of me?"

"You're mine, Violet." He tugged a little, sharp points of pain gathered on my scalp. "I don't like it when people touch my things."

I dropped my keys and used both hands to push at him. Rage painted everything red.

"I'm not yours and I'm sure as fuck not one of your things. I'm a fucking person and you don't get to tell me what to do. Get your godsdamn hands off of me!" I shoved again, stumbling back, when he released me.

He backed me against the door and caged me in with his body and arms. We were both panting with emotion as we glared at each other.

"Why do you have to be so stubborn? This would be much easier if you accepted the truth."

"Why do you have to be so overbearing and insistent? This would be much easier if you went the fuck away."

"Never going to happen, love." With that, he tossed me over his shoulder and started up the stairs.

"What the fuck are you doing?" I squirmed,

but his powerful arms held me around the waist. And there was no escaping the inelegant position.

"You may not like me but you like what I can do to you. So I'm going to remind you of all the reasons you want to keep me around. And I'm going to fuck you until I can erase the image of another man's hands touching you."

I hated that my body reacted to his words. I hated looking forward to whatever he was about to do to me. And I hated the little spark of excitement over his unreasonable and overbearing jealousy.

"Fuck you." I said, for lack of anything better

"That's the plan, love."

Chapter Thirteen

Asmodeus tossed me onto the bed and was on me before the mattress stopped bouncing. He pinned my arms above my head with one hand and bent to kiss me. There was no keeping his tongue out when it demanded entrance.

So, of course, I bit it.

"I love your fangs, love. Feel free to use them anywhere you'd like." As if to demonstrate, As leaned down and sunk his teeth into my neck. I arched against him as pleasure and pain shot through me.

"I hate you." I said, struggling against his grip.

"You hate how much you want me." As gripped the center of my shirt and yanked, his claws cut through the t-shirt with zero effort. He reached for my bra and I screamed.

"Don't you fucking dare. Do you know how hard it is to find a bra that fits? I will cut off your balls." He eyed the garment, clearly considering it anyway. "I'm dead serious."

"As you wish." He yanked down the cup and bent down to take one breast into his mouth. He sucked. Hard.

"Anything else I need to be careful of, or can I deal with these pants already?" His claws tucked under the waistband of my leggings. Before I answered, he shredded the stretchy cotton. I wasn't wearing underwear, as soon as the material gave, I was bare. He used his hand to shove them as far down as he could before using his foot to shove them the rest of the way.

"Those were my favorite leggings!"

"You have more at home."

"This is my home."

"For now." Before I could object again, his tongue was back in my mouth, battling with mine for dominance.

His left hand still had my arms pinned above my head, so I wrapped my legs around his waist and tried to flip him. It did nothing more than make him chuckle into my mouth. He pinched my right nipple.

"If I let you go, are you going to behave?" He rolled my nipple between his fingers before giving it a long, hot lick.

"Probably not."

"Good." He released his grip on my hands. I left them there for a moment while I decided what I wanted to do. I could stop this. Push him away. It would be so easy to do and I was pretty confident he would stop if I said the word.

But was that what I really wanted? I knew

what he could do to my body and I wanted it. My body already craved his touch. I was already wet from the little nipple stimulation.

Something occurred to me. I looked down at the hand gently rolling my nipple as he waited for me to make my move. The claws were gone. In their place were short, blunt black nails tipping a deep red hand.

"Where do your claws go?" I picked up his free hand and ran my fingers over his nails. They felt like nails. There was nothing weird about them. But these nails were definitely not the two-inch claws that tore my clothing off.

"Shapeshifter," he said before he wiggled his fingers at me. "I can change as I need. And I really need those fingers inside of you."

"Well, what are you waiting for?" I arched my brow in challenge. Asmodeus didn't take the bait. Instead, he released my nipple and shifted to where he was straddling me, pinning my legs between his strong thighs.

"You're such a brat, Violet." He eyed me and my pulse sped up. Whatever he was thinking darkened his eyes and flames danced within their depths.

"Do you know what we do with brats in Hell?" He grabbed my hips and flipped me under him until I was laying on my stomach. "We punish them."

The first smack was more of a shock than pain. The second shot through my whole body like lightning.

"Okay, no." I reached back to cover my ass with my hands. He grabbed them in his hand and brought them up to pin behind my back.

"Tell me to stop and I stop. Otherwise, take your punishment like a good girl."

He spanked me again. And again.

He alternated cheeks, turning my ass hot and red. I could feel my pulse in my clit. I squirmed under him to relieve some of the ache, but couldn't get any friction with my legs pinned together between his.

"Stop, enough." I whined when the heat in my cheeks and the ache in my cunt was more than I could take. "Will you fuck me already?"

Asmodeus laughed, releasing my arms and scooting down my legs until he was at my ankles. "Needy, greedy girl. Only the best sluts get off by getting spanked."

"Fuck you."

"Not yet." He bent down and pressed his lips to my right cheek. Then my left cheek. The heat of his mouth was agony on my stinging ass. But the good kind. The kind that had my body aflame.

I was so turned on it took me a moment to notice As spreading my cheeks. It wasn't until the hot press of his tongue against my tight hole that I registered what he was doing.

"That's a no-fly zone." I said, struggling away from him. He didn't release me.

"Only because you don't know how good it could be." He pinned my hips in his hands, his thumbs pressing into my hot cheeks and pulling them open. His hot tongue lapped at me. "Doesn't it feel good?"

Weird, uncomfortable, strange, arousing. Sensations slammed through me as his tongue circled the tight ring of muscle. My pussy was running freely, juices sliding down my clit to pool on the bed.

I was so focused on the conflicting feelings, I was shocked when one, two large fingers slid into my pussy. He thrust and curled, rubbed and stroked, all the while keeping up the steady lapping.

It wasn't enough. There was so much sensation and pleasure it overwhelmed me, but I couldn't get over the edge. I tried to wedge a hand under me to stroke my clit, but he stopped me and pulled my arm out of the way.

"Uh-uh. You come when I say you come." He said the words against my flesh, causing a wave of pleasure. His tongue thrust into me, shocking me. The foreign sensation and the sudden stretch had me backing away from the edge. His fingers pressing into and circling on my g-spot had me right back to it.

He continued that way for what felt like forever. Switching from licking to fucking me with his tongue. From gentle thrusts to hard, fast rubbing. Taking me close to orgasm and then leading me away. Over and over again.

My entire body was damp with perspiration, my limbs shook, my stomach trembled. I wanted, no needed, to have an orgasm like I needed my next breath. I lay there pinned beneath him, at his mercy, panting to catch a breath he would never fully let me recover before pushing me to the edge again.

"Now. Come now." He thrust his tongue into me at the same time he began pulsating his fingers on my g-spot. His other hand came up to press and circle on my clit.

I had no choice but to obey.

It was completely overwhelming. This wasn't a gentle orgasm, a simple release of pressure and pleasure. It was all-consuming. My vision went dark, my breath came in great gasps. Wave after wave crashed over me.

"That's it, my little slut." He said against my hole. "Come for me."

"Too much. It's too much." I gasped. My throat dry and raw.

"You can do it." He thrust his tongue deeper. "Just one more for me."

"No." I shook my head and dropped my face into the bedding. "Can't."

"Yes, you can. I'm not going to quit until you give me what I want." He began to thrust his fingers into me. The sound of my cum filled the room as he sloshed in my soaking cunt. I could feel the sheet beneath my legs getting wet with my fluids.

"Come for me. One more time. You can do it." His movements slowed, and he shifted to position me on my side. He brought one leg up over his shoulder and moved so his mouth wrapped around my overly sensitive clit.

He sucked, hard. Sensation flooded my body, and I had no choice but to give in and give him what he wanted. The orgasm was burning flush through my body, a fire in my veins. It was too much and not enough, and I couldn't get control of it.

By the time sensation returned, As had removed his hand from my pussy to gently rub circles on my stinging ass. He was lapping at my clit in soft, gentle movements as I came down.

"There you are. Such a good little slut." He pulled away from me and I was shocked when he got up and left the room. My body went cold without his heat and, for some reason, I felt like crying.

Stupid. It was just the post-orgasm come down. It had nothing to do with him leaving me without a word.

I was still laying there struggling to get control of my emotions when he returned with a bottle of water and a damp kitchen towel. He cracked the lid and handed me the bottle before using the towel to clean up the mess I'd made of myself. His movements were gentle and kind. It was more after care than any guy had ever shown me, and I didn't know what to make of it.

"Drink." Asmodeus commanded.

The part of me that rebelled at being told what to do was tempted to pour the bottle of water on him. But my throat was raw, my mouth filled with cotton, and I didn't want my bed any wetter than it already was. So, I drank.

"Good girl."

I downed half of the bottle in one go, appreciating the cool water on my parched mouth and throat. And if a little bit of me lit up at the praise, well, that couldn't be helped.

As moved off the bed and stood beside me, eyeing me like a meal. As though he hadn't been devouring me for the last forever.

"Don't even think about it." I moaned, turning over to bury my face into the blankets. I fumbled to put the bottle of water on the bedside table before pulling a pillow over my head. "I'm dead."

"Oh, but what a way to go." As' voice was a rumble of appreciation. His hands came to massage my lower back for a moment before sliding down to rub and smooth over my overly round butt.

"Stop." I swatted at him. My hand landed on a firm thigh. I took advantage of the moment and ran my hand up the thick, muscular limb. Something hard and hot brushed against the back of my hand and I realized he was still hard. While I had come until I couldn't see straight, he was still raring and ready to go.

I shifted my grip to wrap around his hard cock. He froze, standing beside the bed. His cock was so wide my finger and thumb didn't meet around the girth of it. It was long and thick and hot in my hand and I wanted it inside of me.

Releasing him, I flipped over onto my back and shoved the pillow away before looking up at him. Flames danced in his black eyes as he stood over me, slowly stroking his cock.

In that moment, he looked every bit the demon lord he claimed to be. A fierce god people worshiped. He was perfection.

And I wanted to break him.

"Fuck me." I demanded, bringing my hands up to cup my sensitive breasts. "Stop playing with yourself and come play with me instead."

It was a stupid thing to want. I was so over-stimulated and sensitive and soreness was starting to set in. But I couldn't help it. I wanted that gorgeous cock inside of me.

As stopped stroking himself and climbed onto the bed on his knees. He lowered his head to kiss me.

"Admit you're mine," he said against my lips. "And I'll give you everything you're begging for in those big brown eyes of yours."

"Never." I reached up to stroke his cock, circling the head to catch the drop of precum that beaded there. I brought my thumb to my lip, and sucked it off. His nostrils flared and eyes went dark as he watched me.

"Then you can't have my cock." He started to pull away, but I held firm. I raised my head to take him into my mouth. He was so hard and so hot. He tasted spicy, and I wanted more.

I rolled to the side to take him deeper and he

groaned above me. Good. I wanted him as out of his mind as he made me.

Asmodeus allowed me to have my way for a couple of minutes before he broke. He shoved me onto my back and straddled my chest, thrusting his cock in and out of my mouth. He was going a little too fast, a little too deep. I was drooling and gagging. It was angry and obscene.

And I loved every minute of it.

Especially when he leaned back to slide his hand to cup my pussy and grind his palm against my clit. He slid two, then three fingers into me. The stretch was impossible and so, so good.

"When you're done fighting me, I'm going to fill this sweet pussy with my cum over and over. You'll never go without me leaking from you. And you and everyone else will know who you belong to."

I wasn't sure if the sound I let out was a plea or an objection. Everything was too much. He stiffened in my mouth.

Asmodeus swore, and pulled out as he thrust his fingers deep inside of me. I whined at the loss of him and at the nearly painful stretch. He kept thrusting inside of me even as he fisted his cock and began jerking himself off. He covered my neck and chest in his cum. The fluid hot on my skin. I wondered if it would leave red marks on my flesh.

I wondered if I cared.

As' palm ground against my clit as he continued to thrust into me. Just as the last drop of fluid fell from his cock, I went over the edge.

Chapter Fourteen

"You're going to be the death of me, little witch." Asmodeus wrapped his hand around my neck, pressing his cum into my skin.

He wasn't restricting my air. Which was good, because I was still struggling for breath after that last orgasm.

"You've called me that before. I'm no witch. I'm an idiot with a spell book and bad ideas."

As removed his hand from around my throat and lifted his fingers to my lips, he pressed them inside my mouth. He groaned when I licked the pads of his pointer and middle fingers before sucking his cum off of them.

"I've spent every day for millennia listening to idiots with spell books. The witch who owned the book before you was particularly stupid. Which is why I recognized the spell when cast. I knew from the moment I saw you; you would be mine."

I slapped his hand away from me and sat up.

The sheets and blankets were on the floor, so I grabbed a pillow and hugged it to my chest, feeling naked and hating it.

"That's bullshit. You can't see someone for five seconds and decide to keep them. Love at first sight doesn't exist."

Asmodeus sat up too and turned on the bed, sitting with one leg bent before him and the other foot planted on the ground. I waited for him to get up, but he didn't.

He also didn't reach for me. He flexed his hands and his claws extended. I wondered if it hurt when they came out, but I wasn't going to ask. It wasn't the moment. There probably would never be a moment to get all of my questions answered.

"What makes you think love exists at all?" His calm, dismissive tone made my hackles rise.

"I've seen it. I know it's real. Maybe a soulless, heartless, beast like you is incapable of feeling it, but that doesn't make it any less real. Just because I believe in love doesn't mean I believe in love at first sight. That's bullshit. The best you get is lust at first sight, which I find highly doubtful.

"So, why me? Why did you choose me to torment?"

I flung my arms out wide, frustrated and angry. It was the question that plagued me. Why me?

Why was I so unlovable?

Why had I done the stupid spell?

Why had I gotten cursed?

Why would this demon lord choose me?

I hated that I didn't have an answer for any of it. I needed to know. I needed to know why he chose to make me miserable, why he chose to claim me as his?

Why? Why? Why?

"Torment? You don't know torment. I've been tormented for centuries trying to find the right person to be my queen. I finally found her and she doesn't believe in what I am. Not only does she not believe in demons, she doesn't believe in love. She's given up."

That wasn't me. I'd never given up on love. I wanted it. I wanted it so badly I'd cast a fucking love spell to get it.

Except a small part of me was worried he was right. That I had given up on love. That maybe the loss of belief is what led my spell astray. I'd stopped dating in the months leading up to my birthday. I'd only felt lukewarm affection at best for anyone in years. I'd never come close to feeling the love and passion my friends have.

"So, I send my worst demons to her. The low-hanging fruit of demon kind that found themselves on the wrong side of the church. For centuries they'd been of little use to me but now I had the perfect job for them. Luckily for me, I had the perfect ones to put in place to remind the little witch that love exists.

"For months, I watched and waited and prepared and fell a little more in love each day with the sexy, strong, fierce woman who'd called out to the goddess but found her way to me. While I watched her, she watched her friends find love and I can feel her longing. But I wait, and wait, and wait. Until she calls out to me."

"I never called you."

"Didn't you? Didn't you ask for your wolf to get possessed so you could get laid?" He reached out then, catching my hair and running his claws through it. He gently worked at the tangles he put in there with our athletics. "I could have filled the raggedy wolf but where would the fun in that be?"

I closed my eyes as his claws gently scratched against my skull. There was no suppressing my whine when he stopped. But it was only so he could shift us, so I rested against him with my back against his chest before he went back to working the tangles out of my hair and scratching my scalp.

"I have been waiting for you for so long."

He pressed a kiss to my shoulder, and I sighed. But I still didn't, couldn't, believe him.

"You haven't. You picked a random woman screaming at the universe. You don't know the real me."

One hand slid down to my throat, pinning me back against him and forcing my head back. He loomed over me, eyes boring into me.

"I know you, Violet. I know you're strong. Strong enough to stand up to a demon lord without blinking. Fierce enough to keep people in line. Soft and sweet," his hand slid down from my throat, between my breasts, over the curve of my belly to cup my still sensitive cunt. "Your body was made for me."

"One, no. Two, none of that means you know me. Just because you have some magic ability to turn my body into a puddle of goo doesn't mean you know the important things."

His hands went back to detangling my hair, gentle tugs through the strands as he worked the tangles free. I'd have to take a shower before sleep. I was covered in his cum, but it felt nice to be taken care of.

"You mean the way your family doesn't see or appreciate you? Or how you found your real family in your friends? How you work yourself to exhaustion for other people's children while never wanting your own? That you're jealous of the way your friend Clover dresses, but for some reason refuse to dress for yourself?"

My throat went tight at the words. While it was unbelievably creepy that he'd been watching me without my knowledge for months, it was so validating to be seen by someone. Even if that person happened to be a demon lord.

"What if that isn't enough?" I asked.

"It will have to be." He tugged my hair until I was looking up at him again. "Because I'm not going to let you go."

Chapter Fifteen

"I have to return home." As said, playing with the strands of my hair where it fell over my shoulder. My stomach clenched. It was a foreign sensation, and I didn't know what to make of it. "I've been gone longer than I should have."

"What's so important there?"

"I am the lord of seven legions. It is my duty to maintain them. Demons tend to get a little careless when there isn't enough oversight."

"Careless?"

"They're demons, love. I'm sure you can imagine all of the ways leaving them alone could go wrong."

I could. I'd seen enough true crime dramas and watched enough Supernatural to know demons weren't all Johnny Homemaker like the ones my friends found. I just never thought there was someone keeping a leash on them. It went against my understanding of Hell and demons.

Before I could ask about it, Asmodeus dropped a bomb on me.

"I'm taking you with me."

I sat up, the blanket dropped from around me as I shifted to glare at the reclining demon. Nudity meant nothing to me at the moment.

"You're what now?"

"You're coming with me. Our bargain is nearly up and I'm not willing to leave you here."

He reached for me, but I leapt out of the bed. I blindly pulled clothing from the dresser and put them on. Not giving a fuck, I forgot my underwear.

"What are you doing?" Asmodeus said, sitting up. The sheet pooled around his hips, leaving his stomach and chest bare. A sight that would normally give me pause, but I was too angry to be distracted by his physical form.

"I'm going to work. I have a job to do and a little girl who needs to be looked after."

I stormed out of the room and down the stairs, my blood boiling. How dare he assume I would give up my life? That I would follow him blindly into Hell?

"Violet, get back here." the demon yelled, "You're mine and you're coming with me."

The fucking hell I was.

"You're a stubborn, arrogant, unyielding ass." I said, throwing open the door to my house. "I'd say go burn in Hell but you're already doing that! Do whatever you want, you're going to anyway."

"You don't get to walk away from me like

this." Asmodeus roared from inside the house. Unable to come out and scare my neighbors, who were probably enjoying me making an ass out of myself. I knew he could take human form, but I also knew it took a lot of effort to do so. I would be gone before he'd managed it.

"Watch me!" I yelled back, getting into my car. I was backing down the driveway when he came out of the house looking like an Icelandic god. Tall, long blond hair, piercing blue eyes. He stormed into the road and glared at me as I drove away.

Godsdamn asshole for thinking I would be okay with giving up my entire life and living in fucking Hell. Actual fucking Hell. I didn't care I'd be his queen. I had a life, and a job I loved, and friends. I couldn't just walk away from all of it.

I seethed silently all day even as I put on my best happy face for Lily. I blew up the group chat while she played at the splash pad. I mentally listed all of the reasons why Asmodeus was the worst possible thing that ever happened to me.

I was still hot and ready for a fight when I got home that night. The girls had been annoyingly quiet, letting me rant but not offering any feedback. Which I knew meant I was possibly being overdramatic, but it wasn't like any of them lost anything when they fell in love with their demons.

Fell in love?

No, that couldn't be right.

I wasn't in love with the stupid, stubborn demon.

All we did was fight and fuck. That wasn't love.

Was it?

I unlocked the door and stomped in, expecting him to be there and ready to fight with me. Instead, I found my house empty. There were no demon shadows cleaning, no skanky secretary to glare at me. The mess that had taken over my dining room was gone. And so was the giant demon who had been the bane of my existence for the last year.

There was no sign he'd ever been there. Nothing.

I walked upstairs in a fog, trying to figure out the hollow feeling in my stomach.

In the bedroom, I found the first and only sign he'd ever actually been there. The crochet werewolf from Clover sat propped on the pillows in the center of my bed. On its lap was a rolled-up piece of paper sealed with black wax.

Carefully lifting the seal, I unrolled the thick ivory paper and read the broad, loopy handwriting. Then I sat down and read it again. After the third time, I pulled my phone from my pocket and sent a text to the group chat.

Violet: I need someone to take me to Hell.

Chapter Sixteen

"Are you sure about this, Vi? This is a one-way trip. I don't have the power to bring you back." Tight lines surrounded Jax's eyes and mouth as he looked at me. He held a visibly worried Fern's hand as they both tried to talk me out of this.

"I'm sure. As long as you won't get into trouble for helping me. I don't want to ruin anything for you." Given how angry Asmodeus was when I left him that morning, it wouldn't surprise me if he recalled all of the demons he sent before him to punish me and my friends.

There's no way to know who got you there. As long as we're careful of where we land, it'll be okay."

"Vi," Fern said. She didn't need to say anything else. I could read it all on her face. She was worried, scared. She didn't understand and I couldn't blame her. I hardly understood myself.

"He canceled the contract, Fern. Despite

everything between us, despite trying to claim me, he let me go. Shit, he even gave me the name of the human man I was destined for." That little tidbit had made his jealousy and anger over Logan make so much more sense. If I hadn't done the spell, if I hadn't brought Asmodeus into my life, I would have found my way to Logan through normal means. We'd get married and raise his daughter together, and it would have been great. I could see it play out before me easily enough.

Except, even knowing he was the one I was destined for, I felt nothing for him. That vision didn't fill me with excitement. It made me a little sad for the person I was and the person he lost. Logan was a good human, and deserved someone who would love him and Lily with everything she had. I wasn't that person.

I was stupidly in love with an asshole demon.

"Why can't it be enough?" Jasmine asked, logical as always.

"You were happy without Phin," I pointed out. "You were content in your life. Would you give him up now? Would you go back when you have him?"

We both looked toward the demon in question, his red and black form reminding me of Asmodeus. My heart clenched. I wanted to be done with this conversation. But I owed it to my friends. They deserved to know I wasn't being impulsive and making yet another bad choice.

"It's not the same." Jasmine argued.

"Yes, it is. As is stubborn and bossy and overbearing but he cares for me in his own way. He tries to take care of me. He's an absolute idiot but I love him."

"She actually means it." That was Clover. She was looking a little too closely at me. Let her look. I was more certain about this decision than I had been about anything else in my life. "You really love him."

"If love is wanting to punch him in the face at the same time I want to kiss him, then yes."

"Sounds about right." That was from Candy. Her dark violet eyes were alight with humor. While she was the most reserved of the group, you couldn't help but like the demon. "Oof."

Clover elbowed her lover in the side before leaning over to press a kiss on her cheek. They were so damn cute.

"Okay then, let's do this." Jax pressed a kiss to Fern's forehead before reaching out his hand for me. "Whatever you do, don't let go."

"Wish me luck," I said to my friends before grabbing Jax's hand. The next thing I knew, everything went black.

Chapter Seventeen

"Never again. I am never, ever doing that again." I said, bending over and clutching my stomach as I tried to settle my stomach. I was dizzy and nauseated after the trip to Hell. I don't recall anything after taking Jax's hand until I woke up lying on a cold stone floor ready to toss my cookies.

"It gets easier." Jax shrugged. "Come on, I'll take you to the throne room but then I have to leave. I need to get back to Fern."

I followed him through winding hallways and up a neve- ending flight of stairs that had me pausing for a breath at the top. I guessed if nothing else, this trip would get my cardio levels up. Maybe I'd actually close the damn exercise ring on my watch for once.

"Here we are." Jax said, pausing outside a pair of oversized arched doors. "He'll be in there. He usually is. Do you know what to do?"

"Yes. Thank you for bringing me." On impulse, I reached up and pressed a kiss to his cheek. "I'm glad Fern found you. Take care of her for me."

"You worry about yourself. I'll take care of her." He put a hand on the ring of the door and paused. "Be careful, Vi. Asmodeus has never been the most forgiving of demon lords."

I patted his arm and nodded. Knowing full well I was going to ignore his advice. Asmodeus might not be the most forgiving of demon lords, but he was my demon, and I knew how to handle him.

Jax yanked the door open and then vanished before anyone inside could see him. If I didn't know what was at risk for him, I'd call it almost cowardly. But I would never want him to risk himself. Fern needed him too much. And I needed her to be safe and happy. Knowing my friends were cared for made this decision easier.

"Asmodeus, did you seriously think you could get rid of me that easily?" I stormed into the throne room, ignoring all of the demons and humans there. "We had a bargain and you're not backing out."

"Violet," Asmodeus' voice was low, a warning.

"Stuff it," I climbed the stairs to his throne, a little shocked no one tried to stop me. They wouldn't have succeeded, but I kind of expected them to try.

"You don't belong here." The demon lord said, his voice low. Just for me.

"I don't belong anywhere else." I stopped in front of him and planted my fists on my hips, ready for the fight ahead. "We had an agreement."

As stayed sitting, his legs sprawled in what could have been called a lazy and dismissive pose but I could see the tension in him. In the way his hands were fisted on the arms of his chair, in the clench of his jaw.

"And I released you from it. You're free to go live your life as you wish. Go marry the blond and make many obnoxious babies."

"You are such a fucking moron." The gasps rang through the room. I turned to glare at the crowd of people until they shut the fuck up.

"Get out!" As roared. There was a flurry of movement as they cleared out, leaving us alone in the large stone room. As glared down at me, a look that might have frightened me days ago but now had me biting back a smirk.

I took two steps closer, putting myself between his splayed legs. His hands twitched, I knew he wanted to reach out and grab me. It took it as an invitation to drop my hands to his shoulders and climb to straddle his lap.

"What the fuck are you doing?" He didn't grab my hips like I wanted him to, but he didn't shove me off either.

"I'm coming for you." His eyes flashed red. "Do you hear me, Asmodeus? I'm coming for you. Because you're mine."

His eyes were fire when I leaned down to

press my mouth to his. "You're mine. And I am yours."

As snapped. His hands fisted in my hair as his mouth crashed down on mine. The kiss was fierce, intense, brutal. He claimed me with the kiss.

"Mine," he growled, dropping one hand down to my ass to grind me into his rigid dick. "You're mine."

"And you're mine." I gripped his shoulders and swiveled my hips on his lap. He took my mouth in another demanding kiss. Insistent and fierce.

I reached between us to his pants and undid the button. I pulled my mouth away from him enough to issue a demand.

"You're not going to deny me this, not this time."

"I wouldn't dream of it." His hands went beneath my skirt and he snapped the sides of my panties. "You're mine now."

"You idiot, I was all along." I yanked down his zipper and freed his impossibly hard cock.

"You could have fooled me." He groaned the words as I closed my hand around his length. He grabbed my wrist and stopped me after only a moment of stroking him.

I arched my brow at him, and he chuckled. "Such a needy slut."

He dragged a finger along my already damp cleft. A touch so soft it had me arching my hips to beg for more.

"I'm not coming until I'm inside you. And even as wet as you are, you're nowhere near ready for me." He gently circled my clit before sliding his hand down between our bodies and sliding a finger inside of me. His hands were so big, even the one digit was a stretch. "You are temptation incarnate. I'm going to fuck and stretch this pretty pussy until you're able to finally take my cock."

He pulled out, returning with another finger before curling them inside me. His other hand came to rest on my ass, a finger trailing between my cheeks to press against my tight hole. I squirmed, the sensation strange and different but not unpleasant.

"I love that you've never been fucked here. I get the pleasure of teaching you how much fun it can be to have all of your holes stuffed and fucked."

"Later." I growled, grabbing his horns and dragging his mouth down to mine. "Shut up and fuck me already."

"Such a needy slut." As nipped my lip and pulled his fingers out of me. I wanted to sob at the loss. "I believe I promised to worship you like a queen."

Asmodeus stood up with me in his arms and turned to set me on his throne. Strong hands spread me wide, legs over the arms of the throne and completely exposed to him. He dropped to his knees and bowed his head to me.

His tongue was a hot brand against my skin. His groan shuddered through both of us.

"You look like Heaven but taste like sin. I could spend forever between your legs and never get enough."

"As!" It was a whine. A plea. I needed his cock, and I needed it now. I didn't want this slow teasing. I'd waited so long for him and I wanted it so much.

"Patience, love. Patience." I was about to yell at him again, thoroughly impatient, when he bent his head and drove his tongue into me without warning or preamble. It was long and thick and so, so good. But it still wasn't what I wanted or needed.

"As, please." I wasn't above begging. I'd waited for him for so long and I needed to feel him, all of him. "More."

His tongue withdrew from me, only to move up and circle my clit. He slid two fingers inside of me, and then three. The stretch was almost painful, but the pleasure assaulting my clit as he flicked it with the tip of his tongue counterbalanced it. He curled his fingers and at the same time sucked my clit into his mouth. It scraped against his pointed teeth and the combined pleasure and pain and ache had me seeing fireworks.

I was still flying high when I was hauled up out of the throne and found myself straddling Asmodeus' lap.

Spread wide over his sprawled legs and his hard cock between us, I gripped his shoulders. As moved a hand between us to position the head of his cock at my entrance. I expected him to bury himself inside of me, but he teased. He entered slowly, stretching me around him one inch at a time. It was so good. It was almost too much. It was more than I expected and exactly what I needed.

His grip was firm on my hips as he slowly pulled me down his length. I wanted so badly to slam myself down and feel him deep within me but the look of awe on his face was enough to allow him to set the pace. Even if it was almost agonizingly slow.

"So sweet." His eyes locked on mine. "You're taking me so perfectly. What a good girl. What a good little slut. I've been waiting for you forever, my love."

"Good. You're stuck with me." I reached down and pulled my skirt out of the way so I could watch as his cock stretched me wide. "There's no changing your mind now. We're in this together, for better or worse."

With one final thrust of his hips, Asmodeus slid the rest of the way inside of me and we both froze, my eyes flying back to his to see the flames banked there.

"You're mine." He whispered, pressing a kiss to my neck. "There's no going back. Not for you or for me."

"Tell me again in ten years." I challenged him, moving my hips to grind against him. Needing movement. I was so full it almost hurt and sitting there locked in position without movement was slowly driving me out of my mind. "Will you stop being sappy and fuck me already?"

"I'll tell you again in ten years." Thrust.

"A hundred years." Thrust.

"A thousand years." Thrust.

"Time has no meaning for us, my love." Thrust. Thrust. Thrust. "And I'll love you through all of it."

There was something there I needed to think about. Something in that statement needed to be explored but As was moving in earnest now and I couldn't think as he used his grip on my hips to help move me up and down over him. Every downward stroke brought my clit in contact with his pelvis, and I was quickly brought back to the edge.

When he reached between us to circle my clit, I stopped thinking entirely. There was a single thought in my mind as I fell over the cliff.

"Mine."

Chapter Eighteen

"You don't know what you're asking, love." Asmodeus said.

I was sitting at my vanity trying to tame my hair into something presentable after As had completely destroyed it. I was being officially presented to Lucifer and the rest of the demon lords. After a week in Hell, mostly in Asmodeus' bed, it was really starting to sink in. What I'd done and what I'd given up. I turned to look back at As, where he still laid lounging on the bed. What I'd given up, but also what I'd gained.

As spoiled me. He worshiped me. He cared for me and gave me everything I wanted. Everything but this. This one thing I was absolutely determined to have.

"I am asking for you to guarantee my friends' happiness and security. I don't think it's too much to ask." I tucked a strand of hair back behind my ear and picked a pair of diamond studs from the case of earrings.

As had spent most of the year I'd been trying to escape him preparing for me. I had a full cabinet of jewelry, a closet the size of my old bedroom filled with clothing. Some of which I wouldn't be caught dead wearing, but most of it perfectly fit my style. So much of it was the style I'd wear if I had the money to dress however I wanted. As wasn't lying when he said he knew me. He understood me. He accepted me. All parts of me.

"Releasing a demon into the wild isn't something done lightly." As came to stand behind me, wrapping a hand around my bare neck and using his grasp to pull me back against him.

"I'm not asking lightly." I wiggled back against him, feeling his cock between my shoulder blades. I was so going to need a quick shower before we left. "I'm also not going to accept no for an answer. Are they really so terrible they can't be released? Are they going to reign chaos down on Earth?"

As didn't speak. His hand slid down into the gap of my silky robe, and cradled my breast. I knew he was stuck. Either he admitted they weren't the type of demons to cause problems or he admitted to sending evil demons to seduce the most important people in my life.

I tilted my head to the side, allowing As access to my neck. He pressed an open-mouthed kiss to my throat and scraped his teeth over it.

"I can't, love." Another slow kiss. "The demons pose no risk to your friends or the planet at large but releasing them sets a dangerous precedence I cannot allow."

I started to pull away from him, but his other hand came to my neck, holding me in place while he continued to toy with my breast. I hadn't been trying to punish him. I wanted to face him while he explained. Clearly, he had other plans. He usually did. The demon was insatiable.

"What I can do is promise you, an unbreakable bond. They are free to live out their lives as mortals until your friends' time comes. Then they come back to me."

"What about my friends?" I gripped As' wrist where it held me in place. "What happens to them?"

Asmodeus nibbled down my neck to my shoulder. I needed to stop him. We needed to have this conversation, but I needed to get ready to go too. I did not want to officially meet everyone with sex hair. But damn, it felt good.

"It's up to them. They can go wherever they're meant to go or they'll be given a choice to come here." He licked the column of my neck and a chill went through my whole body. "They have to decide for themselves, love. You can't make the choice for them. They're welcome here and I won't leave them to the lower ranks of Hell but it's still Hell."

I had been so isolated with Asmodeus; I wasn't sure exactly what that meant. I needed to figure it out, though. My friends didn't deserve an eternity in Hell if it meant any kind of suffering for them.

"It's good enough." I dug my nails into the wrist I held until he released me enough to turn on the stool to look at him. "For now."

"Violet..."

"Shush. We have thirty minutes before we have to leave." I reached out and stroked the cock standing erect at eye level. "Can't you think of something better to do with your time?"

"You're going to be the end of me, little witch." His hands came to my hair as I took him into my mouth. I popped off his cock to smirk up at him.

"Did you learn your lesson?"

"Lesson?" He echoed stupidly.

"Be careful who you forge deals with. You might be stuck with a pain in the ass for eternity."

"I'll show you a pain in the ass." He hauled me off of the stool and carried me to the bed. "No more deals for me, love. I have everything I want right here."

As he laid me back and spread my robe, I marveled again at the turns my life had taken. A year ago, I'd been desperate enough to be loved that I cast a spell. And maybe I was a bit of a witch because it'd worked. My life was filled with so much love. It may not be the direction I'd planned, but it was perfect.

Absolutely perfect.

Epilogue

"What do we do with it?" Clover, Jasmine, Fern, and I stood around Clover's table, the place where it all began.

Asmodeus had taken me topside, something he really did hate, to celebrate my thirtieth birthday with my best friends. We'd sent the demons off so we could get some girl time in.

In the center of the table was the spell book and the wooden crochet hooks. The cursed objects. As admitted, they were, indeed, cursed. They seemed innocent enough, but I didn't know what to do with them.

"Do we pull a Jumanji and bury them somewhere?" Clover suggested.

"We could burn them."

"Send them to a thrift store? Maybe someone else will have our luck." Fern, ever the optimist.

"Nix that idea. The book is bound to As and I'm sure as Hell not going to let him forge another true love demon deal. He's mine."

"Look at Violet getting all violent." Clover teased.

"Fully prepared to do violence for my demon." I shook my head and wrapped the book and hooks in the black altar cloth we'd used during our ceremony. "Besides, your demons were picked because they're kind of terrible demons. You wouldn't want to meet most of them in a brightly lit room, let alone a dark alley."

I'd spent some time exploring the palace and had run into more than a few demons interested in Asmodeus' human lover. Most of them had been fine but there was a reason I had a bodyguard whenever I left the private rooms and it wasn't only because As was, rightly, afraid I'd get lost.

"I'll take them with me. They can't do any damage down there."

"I still can't believe you live in actual Hell." Fern said, gripping my upper arm. "Can't you live up here with As?"

I shook my head, sad all over again at the loss of my previous life. It was something I struggled with regularly. But as I looked up and watched As talk to the other demons in the backyard of Clover's cottage, I knew it was worth the sacrifice.

He was worth it.

"He needs to be there and I need to be with him." I grabbed her hand and gave it a squeeze. "We have internet service and we can come visit. You're not getting rid of me that easily."

She looked ready to argue some more, but the

back door opened and the demons flooded in. They were all in their human forms, which were physical perfection, but I missed As' other form. He came straight for me and hauled me up against his side.

"I gave you enough time." He stated, he tangled his hand in my hair. "I'm done being out there while you're in here."

"We're done." I leaned my head back and stretched up, waiting for As to bend down so I could kiss him. "You just missed the orgy and the blood sacrifice."

"Haven't you learned your lesson about blood oaths?" He yanked on my hair, bending down to kiss me again. And again.

"Yep." I bit his bottom lip and smirked. "They work out pretty fucking well, don't you think?"

Voices chattered around us, but I focused completely on the demon holding me flush against his body.

"I guess you're right. But no more. Not all demons are as nice as me." I laughed and wrapped my arms around his waist. I'd seen As in action and he wasn't what I would call a nice demon. But he was my demon, and that was all that mattered to me.

"Beast."

"My love."

"Monster."

"My heart."

"Oh, my gods, stop it before I puke!" Clover yelled out, pulling me back and away from my demon. "Let's go get dinner before y'all undress each other in my kitchen and give us all a show."

Everyone paired off and filed out of the room. I picked up the altar cloth with the book and the hooks and put it into my bag. I definitely wasn't risking them falling into the wrong hands.

Not everyone could be as lucky as me.

"Coming, love?" Asmodeus held his hand out for me. I entwined our fingers and squeezed.

"Anywhere you go."

Bonus Epilogue

"Are you ever going to knot me?" My pen scratched across the scroll in front of me and left a dark line across the page. My hand knocked over the inkwell and I swore as I tipped it upright, using magic to burn the ink off of the page.

Fucking Lucifer insisting on the old ways for paperwork. The man controlled the internet and yet we had to write everything longhand. With dip pens. The man would never adapt to the modern era, despite having a hand in creating, and corrupting, so much of it.

I looked across the room where Violet, the love of my life and the bane of my existence, leaned against the doorway of my office. She wore a short little red dress that left much of her lush legs bare and cut low enough to leave her breasts on display. She had her arms crossed under them, lifting them higher and demanding my attention.

"You'll marry me but you won't properly fuck me? It's a little messed up if you ask me."

Oh, she was feeling sassy. I loved it when her claws came out. We'd been together for nearly a year and she still liked to dig them in just as deep as when we'd first met. And I loved every moment of it.

We'd had a mortal wedding ceremony to please her parents before moving to Hell full time. I hadn't understood the point of the ceremony, but it had mattered to her and she'd refused to come with me until completed. She was currently planning Hell's version of a mating ceremony. There was no rush. Everyone knew she was mine and no one would dare touch her.

"No, you infuriating human, I will not." I pushed away from my desk and beckoned her over. She eyed my hand for a long moment, clearly determining how compliant she wanted to be. Eventually, she pushed away from the door and came over to take my hand. "You can hardly take my cock."

"Come on, there's gotta be some portal pussy magic available." She drew my hand to her side before climbing onto my lap to straddle me. It was a tight squeeze in the chair, her legs bent on either side of mine, but I wouldn't complain. Not with her pressed so tight against me.

"Vi..."

"Knot me!" She ground down against me, causing my cock to stir.

"Baby, you've got to stop reading omegaverse

novels. They're giving you unrealistic expectations."

"Never!" She shifted, pushing her boobs into my face. It was a move she knew would certainly catch my focus, but I wasn't letting myself become distracted. "Knot me."

"No." I swatted her ass.

She sat back on my knees and began unbuttoning my shirt. Sharp nails trailed down my chest as she undid each one. My hands gripped her thighs as I waited to see what she did next.

A year with her had shown me all different sides of Violet. I'd seen her soft and gentle. Warm and hot with anger or frustration. I'd seen her happy and mad and sad. Every aspect of her was as fascinating to me as she had been the first time I'd heard her call and decided to answer it. I loved the fact I could never quite figure out what she was going to do. Her moods were quicksilver, and she was quick to change, and it always left me guessing. She was a mystery, and I knew centuries together wouldn't be enough to fully figure her out.

"Are you scared?" She leaned forward and kissed the base of my neck. I tilted my head back to allow her more access. True, she could decide to bite me next. But that was part of the fun.

"Of breaking the most perfect pussy I've ever fucked? Absolutely." I tangled a hand in her hair, currently a dark teal, and held her in place as she pressed hot, open-mouthed kisses to my neck and chest.

"That was almost sweet," she said between kisses. "Full of shit, but sweet."

"My love, if I thought this pussy," I reached under her skirt to cup the pussy in question, "was capable of taking my knot, I would sink it into you in a heartbeat."

I slid her panties aside to sink a finger into her instead. She was already damp and so fucking hot. I couldn't hold back a groan. I stroked deep before pulling out and sinking in with a second finger.

She began to move, using a grip on my shoulders to grind herself down onto my hand as she chased her pleasure. I kept my eyes on her face as she rode me, taking in each flicker of pleasure that crossed it.

"You realize that women shove whole ass babies out of their vaginas every day. Your knot is big but it's no baby's head. It'll fit." She panted the words. Her hands fisted my open shirt, her nails dug into my shoulders as I curled my fingers inside of her and pressed my palm firmly against her clit. I could feel the swollen bud beneath my hand as she neared her peak.

"Why is this so important to you?" I reached between us with my other hand to undo my belt and pants and free my cock. It was so hard beneath her grinding, squirming body. The second she came I was going to bury myself deep inside of her, surround my cock in the wet warmth that was currently clutching at my fingers.

Violet stopped moving and looked down at

me, meeting my gaze. There was lust there but also sincerity, a vulnerability I didn't get to often see from her. I pulled my fingers free of her cunt and cupped her face with my other hand.

"What is it?"

"You're holding back from me." She pushed off of my lap and reached behind her, undoing the zipper on the dress before pulling it over her head and tossing it on the desk. "You've had me in every way possible, some ways I didn't even know were possible. You've touched, licked, sucked, and fucked every part of me but you're holding yourself back. I'm tired of it. I want all of you, As. Every inch of you belongs to me and I want it."

I let out a growl, pulling her back onto my lap. My arms wrapped around her waist and held her close to me as I pressed a kiss to her temple and just enjoyed the feel of her against me. At the same time, my blood blazed and my cock throbbed at this gorgeous, complicated woman claiming me. Even after a year, it was never enough.

I buried my face in her neck and let out a slow breath.

"You have to do exactly as I say," I said to her skin. She squealed, bursting my eardrums.

I wrapped my arms around her tightly and pushed to my feet. If I was going to give her knot, it would not be done in my office where anyone could walk in. I would give her the time and preparation required and I would do it somewhere I didn't risk incinerating someone for seeing my mate naked.

"What are you doing?" Violet asked, wriggling in my hold as I grabbed my suit jacket from the back of my chair and wrapped it around her shoulders, hiding her delicious curves from view even while her mostly naked body pressed against my mostly naked front. Something my cock wouldn't let me forget.

"We're going to our rooms. And then I'm going to fuck you until your legs give out. I'm going to fuck you so well that you'll feel me in your sweet cunt well into next week."

Violet whined against my neck and squirmed in my grasp.

It took every ounce of discipline in me not to shift my hand until I could press my fingers inside of her as we traversed the hallways to our rooms. It was physically painful not being inside of her.

The second we were in our rooms with the door closed behind us, my fingers were inside of her. She screamed at the sudden invasion, the sound, music to my ears.

"That's it, love. Come for me. You'll be doing it all night if we're going to loosen this pussy enough to take my knot." I drove my fingers into her over and over, holding her body pressed against me. I worked her through the first orgasm before dropping her panting body on the bed. I kicked off my shoes before shedding the rest of my clothing and joining her.

"Get on all fours," I ordered, pleased when

she scrambled up on shaking limbs to assume the position I wanted her in. "What a needy little slut."

Violet whimpered but didn't say anything. Some days she'd take issue with being called a slut and would lash out,but other times she loved me calling her exactly what she was. A slut. My slut.

"What a pretty little cunt." I tugged her panties down her legs and left them at her knees, essentially binding her legs into place. Her pussy was so pink and already dripping for me. She would feel so good on my cock if I were to slide into her right then, but that wasn't what she wanted. What either of us wanted.

Because fuck yes, I wanted her to take my knot. I'd fantasized about it for a year. About working her until she was spread so wide that I could work inside of her. I wanted to breed her while buried so completely inside of her. I wanted her spread so wide she would feel empty when she wasn't split open on my knot.

"Please, As. Touch me." She arched her back, pushing her ass and pussy further into the air. With one finger, I slid up from her clit to her entrance. I paused to twirl my fingertip in her cum before sliding back to press against her ass. She shivered under my touch, and more of her sweet scent filled the air as her excitement rose. It was more than a demon could bear.

I bent and closed my mouth over her pussy, devouring her. My tongue thrust into her, and I used a touch of magic to make it grow longer, wider. Enough to stretch her hole around it and to be able to lick against the sensitive spot that made her go wild.

She bucked against my face before reaching an arm behind her to grab my horns and pull me closer. That was my feisty woman. Always so ready to take control of her pleasure.

I moaned against her cunt, flicking the tip of my tongue along her g-spot until she was panting and moaning and shaking in front of me. I pulled my mouth out and shoved two fingers deep inside while moving to suck on her clit. The invasion and the pressure enough to send her over the edge to orgasm.

"That's two. One more and I'll let you have my knot." I promised her, wiping my face on my arm. I moved to line up behind her, pressing my cock against her dripping hole. "Do you think you can be a good girl and come for me again?"

"Would you let me get away with anything less?" Fuck, I loved her mouth. I thrust into her with one jerk of my hips, going all the way deep until her cunt pressed against my knot. Leaning over her, I pressed my fingers, soaked from her pussy, into her mouth.

"Keep up that attitude and I'll have to gag you." I told her, rubbing the pads of my fingers over her tongue before pulling them out and shifting back to my knees so I could drive into her begging cunt.

"Wouldn't be the first time." Violet quipped.

There was laughter in her tone. That itself was a miracle. That she could be riding my cock with hard, deep thrusts and still find humor and laughter.

Still, it wouldn't do to let her get away with giving me attitude. She might stop if I did.

My hand slapped down on her ass. The smack of it rang through the room. Followed closely by Violet's gasp. I gave her a couple of more for good measure, enjoying the way her pussy clenched around my cock every time my hand made contact.

Violet wasn't into pain. She wouldn't thank me if I left long-term marks, but she did like it rough and she liked it hard and she really got off on the unexpected. And I got off on surprising her.

"Touch yourself," I ordered her, returning my hands to her hips to pull her back against my cock until my knot pressed against her splayed lips. "Play with your clit. I want to feel you come on my cock before you take my knot."

It was all the prompting she needed. She lowered herself to one elbow and her free hand shot between her legs so she could rub at her clit. She was already so worked up it only took a minute before she was careening off the edge into orgasm.

I paused to catch my breath. I couldn't let her take me with her. Not this time. I held still as her pussy clenched around me, trying to milk my nearly desperate cock. I clenched my teeth and thought of distasteful things as she panted and sobbed through her orgasm.

Slug demons.

Fungi on pizza.

Violet leaving me.

That last one was enough to shove me back from the edge of my own pleasure. Of all the worst things I could imagine, not having the woman currently spasming on my cock in my life would top the list every single time.

Violet's hand fell away from her pussy and she dropped her head to rest on her arms. Her moans had slowed to soft pants as she caught her breath.

It was time.

I pressed deep, groaning at the feel of her tight cunt pressed against my knot. The knowledge that it would soon be inside her was almost too much. Violet wasn't the first person to take my knot, but everything with her was more intense, better. Violet whined and tensed as I kneed her legs even further apart, opening her more for me.

"Relax, my love. Settle and I'll give you my knot, just like you wanted." I ground deeper, grinding my teeth against the pleasure as my knot eased into her. There was no way I was coming before I was buried fully inside of her.

"Oh, my gods!" Violent panted and squirmed in the grip I had on her hips. "It's so much."

"Too much?" I wasn't fully inside of her yet. Stopping was an option. But fuck me, I did not want to stop.

"Yes," she wriggled against me and pressed tighter. "No, keep going."

It was all the permission I needed. With a grunt, I pushed forward with all of my strength until she opened for me and I was able to squeeze my knot inside her tight channel.

"Fuuuuuuck," I moaned, grinding deeper. "How are you doing, love?"

She'd fallen forward with her arms stretched above her, she gripped the sheets so hard her knuckles were white. Her face was buried in the bed. She let out a high-pitched keening sound but didn't move or say anything else. Her pussy fluttered around me, but I couldn't tell if it was because of pleasure or pain.

"I'm going to need you to use your words, love." I ran a hand up her back to tangle in her hair. I tugged until her head lifted enough for me to see her face. "I'm not moving a muscle until you tell me you're okay."

"Will you just fucking fuck me already?" Her snarl was just what I needed. I couldn't stop the laugh as I released her hair and let her head drop back to the bed. I moved my grip back to her hip and began to rock her back and forth down my cock. I didn't withdraw enough for her to release my knot. Not yet.

The keening was back. A near-constant background sound that mixed with the wet squelch of my cock inside her sopping pussy. We were both panting when her muscles finally relaxed enough to really let me start to move.

My knot pulled out with a near-audible pop, and Violet's keening turned into a moan. The sound turned into a scream when I pushed back inside of her. That scream was enough to send me to the edge. My grip on her hips was brutal as I pulled her back into my thrusts. The tight fist of her cunt on my knot was almost painful in its pleasure.

"Fuck, you're so fucking perfect." I ground deep and her cunt tightened around me and she moaned. "Such a needy little slut, riding my knot like that. Do you want to come, love? Do you want to come while you're stretched around my knot?"

"Please, As please!" She turned her face to look over her shoulder. Her eyes were hazy with lust, but she wasn't there yet. Not quite yet.

I pulled out all of the way, watching Violet drip onto the bed as she bucked back against me. I pressed two fingers deep inside of her, scooping up her cum and coating my fingers with her before I pushed my cock back in. Both of us jerked when my knot slid inside again.

"Maybe even my knot isn't enough for you?" I said, sliding my slick fingers down her crack to her puckered bud. "Maybe you're still not full enough to come. Maybe you really are such a needy little slut you need to be filled in every hole."

I pressed one broad finger into her ass. It passed the tight rim, and Violet jerked hard against me and shuddered. I pulled out and slid both fingers in.

"Do you feel that? You're such a needy slut I didn't even have to get lube. My fingers were soaked with your cum." I twisted my fingers at the same time I ground forward in her pussy. I slid back a bit, just enough to take the pressure off of her cervix. The next time I thrust forward with both my cock and my fingers, I reached around her to press my fingers over her clit.

It was exactly the overstimulation she needed to get there. Violet screamed and jerked against me. Her entire body spasmed as her cunt and ass clenched me so hard my eyes crossed. It was too much for me and the pressure that had been building deep in my balls and tightening at the base of my spine overwhelmed me and I came. The pleasure was pain. The pain was pleasure. Every nerve ending in my body refocused to the feeling of my cock and knot buried deep in Violet's pussy.

When my knot swelled and locked into place in her cunt, my limbs went slack. I dropped over Violet's back with a grunt before wrapping an arm around her middle to turn us to lay on our sides, my cock stuck firmly in her pussy. I ran my hand down her arm and slid it over her belly to cup her pussy, my fingers splaying around my cock.

"How are you feeling, my love?"

"I can't feel my legs." Her voice was still

dazed and a little shocky. "You'd tell me if they fell off, right?"

"They're still there." I released her pussy to smack my hand down on her ass. We both gasped and moaned when the movement made her clench down on me. "Fuck woman, you have to stop doing that or we'll never make it out of this bed."

"That's okay. I am pretty sure you killed me." She snuggled back against my chest with a soft sigh. She linked our fingers together and rested our joined hands against her stomach.

"Oh, but what a way to die." I didn't bother to point out that she was already in Hell and that after our bonding ceremony, she would be immortal. My mate in every way.

"What a way to die." She wriggled a little bit. "Are you going to let me off of you anytime soon?"

"I thought you read Omegaverse books, love. Don't you know you've gotta wait for the knot to deflate? I'm afraid you're stuck with me." I used our joined hands to pull her closer to my chest, curving around her where we lay.

"Okay, I have one question."

"Only one. That's so unlike you." She ignored my nonsense.

"How the fuck do Omegas get anything done?"

Acknowledgments

Dear Reader,

Thank you for coming on this wild journey with me. If you would have told me a year ago I'd be publishing a four book series in the next year I would have laughed you out of the room. But here we are, a complete series of novellas.

And this series wouldn't exist without you. When I wrote Corny it was a manic joke stemming from a Twitter conversation about a crochet bootylicious candy corn. I never expected it to bring me here.

I came to monster/sentient object romance as a completely new person. I knew some authors as a fan under another name but no one knew Sabrina Cross when I stumbled onto the scene. And yet they opened the doors and accepted me with enthusiasm I never expected.

This book exists for the readers and authors I've met in the last year. It exists for every reader who messaged me, tagged me, talked about my books on socials. For every reader who left a rating or review. To every author who kicked my ass when I wanted to quit.

Thanks for coming with me on this weird journey. It wouldn't exist without you.

All my love,
Sabrina Cross XO

About the Author

Sabrina Cross (she/her) is a neurospicy 80's baby from the middle of nowhere Michigan, where she still lives with her cat. She came into her monster romance era early when she fell in love with Beast from the 1997's X-Men animated series. After discovering sentient object romance in early 2023, Sabrina decided to embrace what she calls her 'Hold My Beer' style of writing and gave into the lifelong dream of being an author. When not writing weird monster/sentient object smut, Sabrina can be found hanging out on social media (@authorsabrinacross), reading, or hoarding office supplies.

Also by Sabrina Cross

Yarn & Monsters Series

A True Love Spell Gone Wrong...

When four friends perform a true love spell, things go terribly wrong. Now they're locked into a deal with the devil and have only a year to find love and happiness or their souls are destined to face the flames. Armed with a demon guardian; Clover, Jasmine, Fern, and Violet are determined to beat the devil and save themselves. Except, this curse might be the best thing that's ever happened to them.

Corny: A F/F Candy Corn Romance

A True Love Spell Gone Wrong...

A Demon Fairy Godmother?

Her very soul on the line. Can Clover still find true love or is she destined to face the flames alone?

Snuggle: A M/F Demon Teddy Bear Romance

A True Love Spell Gone Wrong...

Jasmine is too busy to go to Hell and she's definitely too busy for demon antics. But when her demon "Fairy Godmother" shows up, everything is on the line. Does she have what it takes to get out of the Devil's bargain or is she doomed to face the flames?

Tangled: A M/F Friends-To-Lovers Sentient Object Romance

A True Love Spell Gone Wrong...

Fern is going to Hell. Not metaphorical Hell but actual, physical Hell. But there's one thing she needs to do before she goes. An item she desperately needs to scratch off the bucket list. And she's hoping the demon sent to guard her will be willing to help her out.

Knotted: A M/F Demon Werewolf Romance

A True Love Spell Gone Wrong...

Violet was no witch but that didn't stop her from trying to use magic to find love. When the spell backfired and left her and her friends bound in a deal with the devil, Violet vowed to find a solution. Now, with less than two months until the deal comes due and zero leads, she's facing the fire. The fire comes early in the form of a great black beast in her bed. Does Violet find the love she's been looking for or does Hell claim her soul?

Light Me Up

He was the first man to ever turn me on. When he flipped my switch and lit me up that first time, I knew he was it for me. There would never be another.

Pounded by the Pommel Horse

Elena loves being on top. When the elite gymnast is challenged to defeat her gym rival on the pommel horse, she's up for the task. But is she up for the ride when the pommel horse shapeshifts into a man? A very, very naked Man?

Christmas with the Monster

He's Got a Package for Her... Devynn expected her first holiday without her kids to be difficult. But nothing could have prepared her for what she found under the tree just after midnight.With the help of his magic sack, the furry, green giant promises Devynn all kinds of pleasure. But would one night with the Christmas monster ever be enough?

Sentient Pen15 from Outer Space

Liam had spent a lot of his childhood obsessed with the legends of the local mines. The abandoned tunnels underground had driven dozens of workers insane and young Liam was desperate to get to the bottom of it. But he found more than he bargained for down there.

Infected by parasitic space mold, Liam has held himself away from relationships for years. When things spark between him and the girl next door, he has no choice but to reveal the truth: his manly appendage is also the bane of his existence.